This book is dedicated to Trixie Madell, my curious friend.

The KitKat Chronicles:

Kit Maxwell,
Curatore di Mondo

Timothy Noel Harris

TORCELLO EDITIONS • NEW YORK

Published 2018 by Torcello Editions
torcelloeditions.com

Book design by Tara Key/Motorific

ISBN: 978-1-7325364-1-8

To Tim—
With love,
Tara Key

Timothy Noel Harris

To Tim,
With us,
Your [illegible]

TABLE OF CONTENTS

I

Venice: The Other Side of the Canal
9

II

Kit's Roman Holiday
39

III

Paris: The Princess and the Snail
67

IV

Barcelona: Kit Up, Up and Away
89

I

Venice: The Other Side of the Canal

1

"Mama, I want to go for a walk!" Her mother grimaced.

"You know I can't go out right now. Your father and I are making dinner for the whole crowd."

"I don't need you! Just let me go out. After all, I'm almost 10!" Her mother studied her warily.

"Oh, all right, but don't go far, you know how easy it is to get lost here. If you go too far, you'll never make it back. And don't fall in any canals and drown. I wouldn't let you do this in Brooklyn. But the biggest thing to fear here is being trampled by a tourist group. Do you have your phone?"

She nodded and gave her mother a hug and then scampered out the door and down steps and steps and steps, five flights all the way down to the heavy wooden door. She activated the inside buzzer and pulled as hard as she could to swing open the gate to the outside world.

The sun lit up her face. She staggered into the street and blinked.

She walked by the building that looked like the Flatiron in New York and crossed the bridge over the canal. Her father and she had gone down this lane before to buy pasta and cheese.

She retraced their steps, turning right and then left, to enter a narrow lane opening up into a wide campo ahead. She ran her fingers along the rough brick of the wall of a building her father had told her was older than the discovery of America. She felt the cobblestones through her sneakers at the same time.

The window of a food shop scrolled by her on the right with an array of exotic-looking paper sacks of pasta: fusilli, cavatelli, rigatoni, spaghettini. Then she moved to the other side of the street and peered into the paint shop. Powders of 100 different colors presented a rainbow grid of pigments. Her father had bought her a paint box here the day before yesterday.

She started when the proprietress noticed her and yelled out the door in English, "Kit! Are you enjoying your paints?" She smiled and nodded with a wave and the best *"Si signora"* she could muster.

At the end of the *calle*, she stepped around the Campo de Morti, the former graveyard where the pavement is raised a foot higher and forms the patio for a restaurant. Her dad told her about this and she shivered as she thought about the bodies with the plague dumped and sealed up down there. She thought that the tourists eating there knew nothing about this, and she decided she wouldn't tell them.

Bursting out of the dense cluster of narrow Venetian lanes, she found herself in the wide expanse of Campo Santo Stefano, she remembered the name, and turned left up into Campo San Angelo. She looked at the canal running by the campo, with the satisfaction of knowing that it ran right under the church of Santo Stefano. None of the tourists flowing through the lane between the campos knew they were paralleling the underground canal, nor did they know about the dead bodies around the corner; but she did because her father had told her so.

She circled the booth selling bags made by prisoners from the local prison under the brand "Male Fatte." She wondered if the woman working there had been in prison. Could she have killed someone?

The top of the campo funneled into a narrow lane and she contemplated this for a moment, but realized she had never gone this far from the apartment. So, she turned around and skipped back into Campo Santo Stefano. From here she knew exactly what turns to take to get back to her family.

Instead, she headed south across the wide expanse of stones and by the wellhead in the middle. She watched a man throwing a whirlybird thing way up in the air like 40 or 50 feet. It always seemed he would lose it or send it careening into an outdoor café, but he never failed to be there when it fell back to earth, catching it in his hand. "Look, *mira*, *regardez*," he said. "*Cinque* euros, five euros." She ran away and around the church of San Vidal at the bottom of the campo.

A woman played on a group of wineglasses, rubbing the rims to make different tones. The glasses had different amounts of water in them. A crowd of people circled around the performer and dropped change in an upside-down hat. Just beyond, Kit saw the big wooden bridge that crossed the Grand Canal. She danced up onto the bridge and took in the view of the boats gliding by underneath: gondolas, water taxis, *vaporetti*, or water buses, working boats hauling everything. Tourists thronged either side taking pictures of themselves with their selfie sticks. A couple seemed vexed that they couldn't get a good shot. Kit shrugged and said, "I can take it. I know how." They handed her their cellphone, riveted by her authoritative tone, perplexed by her age. She framed them beautifully against the sky and water, touched the screen for focus, clicked off two photos, and handed back the phone. They stared at her in amazement. *"Mille grazie!"*

She rolled her eyes and ran to the other end of the bridge. There, she recognized the art museum they'd visited the day before and the boat landing where they'd gotten off the *vaporetto*. She was proud of her sense of orientation.

But she followed the momentum of people moving down a narrow lane to the right of the museum. As she crossed several bridges over canals, and made turns and switchbacks, her heart thrilled with being a little lost, a little out of her element. She challenged herself to remember every twist and turn, but being a brave girl, she enjoyed knowing there was a little too much for her to remember. She was confident she could retrace her steps, back to the museum, over the wooden bridge, around the church, across the campo.

Coming along the side of a canal, she followed the flow of the crowd under an arch and into a broad campo with a church on her right. The people streamed out of the campo at the far left and she followed them past a barge full of beautiful vegetables for sale: yellow peppers, melons, different colors of radicchio. She knew about Castelfranco radicchio, Treviso radicchio, and Chioggia beets because her father had showed them all to her. She considered herself an accomplished chef.

She headed over the bridge by the vegetable barge humming

some country music to herself. She emerged into another campo which went farther than she could see. Clouds passed over the sun and the campo darkened in shadow.

Around an old brick building in the center of the campo were some wooden stands selling something and she approached. The stands were dripping with melting ice and the odor of the sea was mingled with a stronger smell. She saw the full-length bodies of whole fish with blue-green scaly hides. The largest fish of all peeked over the edge of the wood and stared into her face with one huge dead eye. She shivered.

A seagull dove into the campo with a determined shriek, sending meeker pigeons scattering everywhere, and the fishmonger, covered in stained overalls, menaced the bird with a cudgel. *"Va via, basta, vola!"* he yelled, glaring at Kit.

The sky darkened some more, and she thought about her papa and mama preparing dinner, cutting vegetables and setting the table. The wind blew up and the fishmonger started to dismantle his stand, throwing fish carcasses into coolers of ice.

Church bells began pealing above her head from several directions at once, and Kit backpedaled. She turned and ran as drops of water began to dapple the cobblestones. She ran back to the bridge that entered the campo as the sky poured forth its excess moisture in punishing sheets of water. She ran over the bridge looking for cover. She turned right along the canal away from the vegetable barge and took cover in the doorway of an old Venetian house.

She cowered there, crouching, with water streaming down her

face. Some familiar music came to her ears. "A coat of many colors…" Turning to hear it, she bumped into the door with a loud thunk. Leaning against the heavy door, she looked at the pelting rain and wondered how she would get back. She closed her eyes as water dripped down her nose and into her mouth. Her clothes were completely soaked.

She was dreaming something about school in Brooklyn, about the birds in the Botanical Gardens, she was falling backwards down, down, down…

She awoke with a start. The door creaked open loudly, and she fell back into air. Her head landed by a pair of gray-socked feet. *"Qui et tu?"* a man's voice said. She looked up into a mane of white hair. *"Dove sono tus padres?"* he asked. *"Parle italiano?"*

"English," she said.

"Come, come in from the rain." He handed her a piece of cloth. The door swung shut and made a loud thump like a refrigerator closing. She dried her face.

"I saw her!" she said.

"Dry off."

"I saw her!"

"Who?"

"I saw her!"

"Who? Maria, my wife? She just went out, at just the wrong moment."

"I saw Dolly! Dolly Parton."

"Oh yes, Dolly Parton. Dolly. Did you see her in Venice?"

"No, in Forest Hills, Queens."

"Ah, Queens, in New York. Do you live in New York, in Queens?"

"No, in Brooklyn."

"Oh, I see, but you went to Queens and you saw Dolly Parton. Was she walking down the street?"

"No, silly, she was playing that song, 'Coat of Many Colors.'"

"Oh she was? Walking down the street playing 'Coat of Many Colors.'" He smiled.

"No, no, she was onstage, in concert at Forest Hills Stadium."

"Oh, in concert."

"And I can play that song, too."

"Oh, you can?" Just then, the door clicked and swung inward. A tall, white-haired woman entered, dripping wet.

"Ludovico! Que disastre! Qui e questa? O Ludovico!"

"Ah Maria, welcome home. This is my new friend. She knows Dolly Parton."

"Well, I don't know her," said Kit.

"This is Maria, my wife. But she doesn't speak English. And your name is . . ."

"Kit."

"Kit, pleased to meet you, Kit. She is Maria. I am Ludovico."

"Maria, Lu-do-vi-co." She shook hands with both of them.

"Bene, bene," said Maria. She grabbed the rag from Ludovico and wiped off Kit's hair and her own. She grabbed Kit's hand and led her up some stairs. Kit saw easels and canvases everywhere as she left the ground-floor room. Dolly's voice grew fainter as she reached the top of the stairs. Maria pulled her into a bathroom and handed her a proper towel. *"Que bella,"* she said, looking down at Kit. She disappeared around a corner and came back with a T-shirt, some trousers, and socks. *"Kit, vesti,"* she said. In English, she said, "I dry."

With the oversize pants and T-shirt on, Kit emerged with her wet things and handed them to Maria, who threw them in the dryer. Kit knew this was kind of a luxury, even though they had one in their apartment, because many people in Venice hung their laundry out on a line overhanging the streets. *"Las zapatas,"* said Maria and pulled a luxurious pair of red socks onto Kit's feet. Then she grabbed her by the hand again and led her down into Ludovico's studio. *"Io prendere delle te,"* she said and left.

"Are you warm, Kit?" said Ludovico. "Maria will dry your clothes. She will bring us some tea."

"OK."

"Are you staying around here? Where are your parents?"

"Over the bridge."

"The Rialto?"

"No, the big wooden one."

"Ah, yes."

"Are you an artist?" said Kit, looking around the studio at canvases stacked against the wall, jars of paint on several tables, shelves of art books and vinyl records lying at not-so-neat angles on a bunch of shelves.

"Some would say I am," he said. "I made a big sculpture of a horse once. It is in Chicago. Have you been to Chicago?"

"Yes."

"Oh, you are a world traveler. How old are you?"

"Nine."

"Well, I am 85 years old. Have you seen the horses of St. Mark's?"

"Yes!"

"Well, I modeled my horse after those. But now I am a painter."

"Do you have a gallery?"

"Yes, would you like to see it? I can take you there."

"When?"

"Say, tomorrow, when it's not raining." Maria brought in a tray with a teapot and three cups. *"E decaffeinatto per la ragazza?"* said Ludovico.

"Claro!" said Maria, taken aback that he could consider that she would give caffeine to the little girl. She poured three cups and gave one to Kit.

Ludovico looked at Kit hard, their eyes locking for a long moment. "You paint?" he said.

"OK." She shrugged. He set up an easel in front of her, gave her a brush, and a palette with a variety of colors already splotched out on it. He moved gingerly, using a cane to get up.

"I'm working on the Salute," he said. "You know it?" He turned a large photo of the domed church so that both of them could see it.

"Yes, at the end of the Grand Canal."

"You can sketch first if you like, and then paint it in." He handed her a box of pencils. "I like to work until I get it right, looking just like it is, then I add something that isn't real, maybe, or maybe it is." Kit studied the photo and sketched. She looked over at Ludovico's canvas and frowned. She watched as Maria headed upstairs, her long legs, her short skirt, and high heels not fitting, well, her husband's age.

The pair worked in silence, the old man and the little girl. Every twenty minutes or so, Ludovico put a new album on the turntable. After a while, Kit had a good image of the main features of the church. She like the way it just kind of floated in space without much relation to anything around it. She began to fill in patches with paint. Ludovico looked over at her and she was staring at his face.

"What?"

"Nothing." They worked on without talking. After a while Maria came back down and announced that the clothes were dry.

"Well, Kit, I guess you should go find your family. It has stopped raining. Do you know the way back to your place?"

"Mmmm, it's over the bridge."

"Is it near Santo Stefano on the other side?"

"Yes! Campo Santo Stefano," she said with an exaggerated Italian accent, or at least one that sounded exaggerated in her little New York girl voice. "I can get home from there."

"Maria will walk you. You see, I no longer walk too well. But she is younger, and an athlete. But first go upstairs, and put on your dry clothes." Maria led her away. Lucovico glanced over at Kit's canvas and started. There was the church of the Salute, expertly drawn while floating in space above a sheen of water. Rising over the steps in front of the façade was a face – Ludovico's face, with his white hair and his penetrating eyes, looking back at him. He blinked.

Kit came bouncing down the steps in her jeans. She had neglected to change out of Maria's silky red socks which were big and floppy on her. "Why don't you keep those?" Ludovico said, and Maria nodded. "We'll keep yours, so you'll have to come back." Kit sensed she was making a good deal for her cheap white cottons.

She put on her shoes. Maria swung open the heavy wide door and grabbed her by the hand. Kit looked fiercely at Ludovico and said, "See you tomorrow."

As they walked past the vegetable barge and around through the Piazza San Barnaba, Kit had to reach up to hold Maria's hand. Kit kept looking up at her beautiful face with abundant gray/blond hair cascading around it. Her skin was old like her grandparents', but her skirt was way shorter than her grandma or her mom would wear. Maria's heels clicked on the stones through San Barnaba as the girls working at Ai Artisti café shouted, *"Ciao, Maria! Dove e Ludovico?"* They passed under the arcade and over the bridge, turning left and right before emerging at the Accademia Bridge in front of the museum. Maria's hand held hers tightly. It was soft to the touch. Kit was puzzled at how old Maria was. She couldn't figure it out.

They threaded their way through the tourists on the bridge and walked around the church to emerge in Campo Santo Stefano.

"I know where I am!" Kit shouted. As Maria bent down, Kit kissed her on the cheek and bounded off before the older woman could protest. *"Grazie, Maria! Domani!"*

"Que bella!" Maria shouted as Kit trailed off into the distance. Kit made her way expertly down the lanes that led to their apartment. She thought of several explanations for where she had been, but when she came in, her parents were having cocktails with her aunt and uncle and her grandparents. They all greeted her with pleasure and didn't demand any explanation for her absence.

"Did you get wet, Boo?" her father asked.

"No, I waited under a roof." Suddenly, she remembered her elegant red silk socks and jammed her fists in her pockets so her jeans would stay down over her shoes.

"Great, we'll have dinner on the way in a half-hour. Why don't you go clean up?"

2

The next day, most of the family was taking a boat trip to Murano, but Kit didn't feel quite well enough to go. She said she'd just stay in and rest, maybe go for a walk. Her parents were worried about her, but acquiesced, gave her a key, and told her she could go down to the corner market if she needed anything. "Don't go too far and call my cell if you need anything," said her mom.

Once the other eight of them had left, Kit waited exactly thirty minutes to see if they had forgotten anything and were coming back. Then she tucked the key in her pocket and bolted out the door, down the five flights of steps and out into the stones of Venice. She ran and skipped through the Campo Santo Stefano, over the Accademia Bridge, down through the series of canals and bridges, confident that she knew her way.

When she was approaching the arcade leading into the Piazza San Barnaba, two girls, one her age and the other younger, were kicking around a ball. The younger one kicked the ball toward Kit. It rolled to her feet, and she expertly shot it back with the inside of her right foot. *"Vuoi giocare?"* shrieked the older one in Italian, pointing at the ball. Kit looked on in bafflement. The girl approached and said in her best English class voice, "You play? What … is … your … name? Mine is Kat. She is Elisabetta."

"I am Kit." She hesitated. "But I can't play right now. I have to go meet someone." Elisabetta looked at them from twenty feet away with the ball in front of her. Kat shook Kit's hand. Then Elisabetta kicked the ball, sending it in an upward arc toward them. It went high over their heads, and they watched it frozen at the apex above them for a fraction of a second before it came down and bounced off the low stone wall between the *fondamenta* and the canal and went on a lower arc into the murk of the water with a splash.

While Kat yelled at Elisabetta, Kit suppressed a laugh and went running down across the bridge to the other side of the canal where four steps led down to a landing. From there she could just reach the ball. She shook off the water and brought it back around. "Here," said Kat, grabbing the ball, and took it over to the spigot where people filled their water bottles. She rinsed off the ball and shook it off. *"Tu mane,"* she said and indicated that Kit should wash her hands.

"Thank you," Kat said in English, and gave Kit a kiss on the cheek. Kit waved goodbye, and proceeded through the arcade, across the piazza, beyond the vegetable barge, and reached Ludovico's door.

Some rock music was playing. She banged on the door. "Ludovico! Maria!" The door swung open and Ludovico stood there with a brush in hand.

"Ah Kit. Hello, would you like to go see my gallery?"

....

With his right hand, Ludovico held Kit's left hand. With his left, he steadied himself with his cane, and used it gallantly to clear the way for Kit's path through the pedestrians, like a medieval swordsman wielding his weapon, though he didn't hit anyone. They walked across the piazza where the girls working at the Ai Artisti café yelled at Ludovico. *"Ludo, dove e Maria? Qui e su novia?!"*

Ludovico smiled. "Kit! *Americana!* Pretty cool, huh?" he said in English. They walked down to the vaporetto stop at Rezzonico. Ludovico walked past the machine where you punched your ticket.

Kit stopped him and said, "You have to pay!" But Ludovico said, "It's OK. I am old and you are young," and led her out onto the boarding dock. The boat came and the woman sliding open the gate greeted him. "Ludovico!"

After stopping at the Accademia Bridge stop, they neared the Salute. "Look," said Ludovico, "your painting." Kit looked at the grand church at the end of the Grand Canal just before the point leading into the basin of St. Mark. She looked up at Ludovico's wizened face, at his noble head. She looked back at the Salute. She thought of Mount Rushmore.

They got off the boat at the San Zaccaria stop and waded through the crowds on the Schiavone. He pulled Kit down a side lane and into the Green Bar. "I've got to get an espresso," he said. "Do you want to get a Coke?" Kit said OK. "If you stand at the bar, you pay half price," he said. "And if I sit down, it will be hard for me to get up." The barman poured a little glass bottle of Coca-Cola over ice in a little glass for Kit. He set up a *ristretto* espresso for Ludovico, who downed it in one sip. *"Corretto,"* he said, and the barman poured a clear liquid into his coffee cup.

"What's that?" said Kit.

"Grappa, it's made from grapes."

"You're having a drink?" Kit said incredulously.

"Well, it's a *corretto*, that means it corrects the effect of the coffee."

"You're having a drink!" She punched him in the arm, hard.

"Ow!"

They proceeded into the throngs in St. Mark's Square and under the arcade on the long side, passing a quartet playing on a stage at the café there. A woman played the clarinet. People fed the pigeons and ran around laughing. Ludovico grimaced at all the people there and entered a storefront with an art gallery. "Here we are. I need all these tourists to buy some of these paintings!"

"Did you do all of these?"

"Yes, I did. Hello Giorgio, this is my friend Kit. I've come to show her around."

"Ludovico! So good to see you. Hello, Kit, with pleasure. Ludo, we have sold a painting to a buyer in California. I have money for you."

"Which one did I sell?"

"The one with the submarine."

"Ah, Kit, come take a look. Someone paid some money for my painting. They will for yours, too." Kit looked around wide-eyed and couldn't believe all the paintings Ludovico had made. He led her to a large canvas of the Piazza San Marco. The church, the Campanile, the Clocktower, the arcades all around were painted expertly. Arising in the middle of the square was the scope of a submarine with the whale-like mass of the hulking boat beginning to emerge through the cobblestones. Kit gasped.

"Did that really happen?"

"Well, since you are my friend, I'll tell you, that I made it up. But you never know," he said vaguely. He paused. "Under the Salute there are over one million wooden posts like telephone poles sunk into the mud, so that the church won't sink. But you never know over here. But a boat would have to avoid that." The gallery owner gave Ludovico an envelope. "Great! I can take my girlfriend to lunch!"

They walked around to Rosa Salva, where he ordered them some sandwiches. "Would you eat *tono olive*? Or perhaps, *tono uova*? That's tuna with olives or tuna with egg."

"Tuna with olives!" Kit said. This time they sat down, and ate *tramezzini* with white bread with the crusts cut off. As she munched her sandwich, Ludovico said, "I want to take you somewhere else nearby: the church of San Zaccaria. They left and walked to the left of the San Marco church and down a lane into the courtyard in front of a church. Some boys kicked a soccer ball off the multilayered façade on the front of the church. A priest emerged from the church and chased them away.

"Come," said Ludovico. "This is a working church, not just a museum, they still say mass here." They entered and he took her up on the left to the altar with the big painting of the Holy Family by Giovanni Bellini. He let Kit study it for a while, then pointed to a door on the right side of the church. A man there was taking money to enter the sacristy and the crypt, but he waved them through. Ludovico ignored the paintings and statues there and showed Kit a stairway behind the altar which led downstairs into the crypt. There were some faded frescoes on the walls. A rope stopped Kit from walking into a pool of water, which took up most of the space.

"Is this from the lagoon?" she asked. He nodded.

"It's all under the city. Here in this crypt, 100 nuns died trying to escape a fire that burned down the church in the ninth century. This is like a memorial to their sacrifice."

Kit looked at the water in the pool and the walls. She thought about the submarine sitting behind the wall, navigating between the telephone poles in the dark. She thought about the Venetian girls' ball bouncing into a canal and off the top of a submarine.

3

Kit was dreaming about the covers. She was dreaming about how they weren't covering her completely. "Hey, where did those come from?"

"Cool, where did you get those? I want them." Kit woke with a start and blinked. Her feet were sticking out from under the blanket, and her cousins were examining Maria's red socks.

"Those are amazing. They must be silk!"

"Hey Kit, where'd you get the socks?" Half awake, she blurted out, "My boyfriend gave them to me." Then, she thought better of that and added, "Well, my boyfriend's wife."

"What, your boyfriend?"

"His wife?" The cousins were incredulous as Kit came to full consciousness and regained her wits. She had never had a boyfriend, but her cousins both had, sort of, had boys who were more than friends.

"Oh wow, I was dreaming," said Kit. "I was having a crazy dream about Venice."

"Well, where did the socks come from? Not out of the dream!"

"Oh, I got them from a guy on the street," Kit neatly improvised, thinking quickly that he just maybe couldn't be found again. It occurred to her that the guys on the street only sold expensive leather bags, toys, and selfie sticks, but she carried the lie off pretty well. She even convinced herself that it wasn't really a lie, as she really didn't want to lie to her cousins, that Ludovico could be considered a guy on the street. And she had said "got them" rather than "bought them," and *that* was accurate.

"How much?"

"Oh, I forget. Not much."

"Well, they're really nice. Show us where he is." Kit, of course, couldn't show them that, but she did have a strong desire to spill her secret relationship, to let her cousins in on the cool stuff happening to her.

"I'll show you later," she said.

....

She practically dragged the two of them on her now-familiar

route, holding each by the hand. To Campo Santo Stefano, turn right, go around San Vidal, cross the Accademia Bridge, turn right in front of the museum, turn left, cross two bridges. Here, two Italian girls playing with a ball, yelled, "Hallo, Kit!" The cousins looked at each other, then at Kit. "Who are you?" they said together.

They went under the arcade into Campo San Barnaba. A woman at the café Ai Artisti shouted, *"Ciao, Kit, dove et tu novio?"* and laughed. Kit steered her cousins down the *fondamenta* past the vegetable barge right up to Ludovico's door. There was no light inside. There was no music. She banged on the door. There was no sound. She banged furiously on the door with tears sprouting in her eyes, shouting one word for each bang. "Why? Aren't? You? Here?!"

Kit led the cousins into the Campo San Margarita and pointed at the open-air fish market. Then she took them to Al Volo pizza for an almost-NY-style slice, into the stationery store where she bought them notebooks, and to the Doge gelato stand for a cone. Kit paid for everything which came to about ten euros total, acting all the while like she had brought them all the way there to see the wonders of Campo San Margarita.

She loved her cousins very much and wanted to impress them. Once again, she improvised brilliantly. "I don't know where the guy with the socks went. I got them over there." She pointed vaguely over at the canal with the vegetable barge as if she'd been pounding on a door and practically crying because She! Couldn't! Find! The! Sock! Vendor!

What she said had the virtue once again of being almost true, as she did get the socks "over there" at that door. The cousins were a little concerned. "It's OK Kit," they said. "Thank you for all the presents. It's been a really nice walk. I'm sure we'll find the guy. I can't believe all the friends you've made. And in Italian! Are you OK?"

Kit perked up and led them back to their neighborhood. What with her skipping the boat ride to Murano and this strange walk, the cousins remained a little worried about her.

Three days later, they would be baffled again by her behavior. No one knew that for three days straight she had slipped away and made the trip over, only to find Ludovico's door dark and silent, as if he had disappeared off the face of the Earth. She was worried that he might have died; he was much older than her grandma and grandpa.

They had reservations to eat out in the local trattoria that night. Her papa and mama had been shopping at the Rialto market every day and cooking every night, but as their visit neared its end, they were ready to be waited on.

All nine of them went out together, dressed, more or less, for dinner. They entered the Ristorante Tiziano and were shown to the large table at the back. They were sitting there having a good time studying the Italian menu playing the game of not resorting to asking for an English one, when Kit looked up with a stunned expression like she had seen the ghost of a dead doge. "Kit, what's the matter?" said her mother. She was staring at a picture framed on the opposite wall.

"I did that," she stammered. "I did that."

"You did what?"

"I did that painting. I made it."

"Kit, come on, what do you mean?"

"I did it." Her father called over the proprietor.

"What is that picture there, please?"

"Oh, we just received that today from our favorite artist here in Venice. He sends us his stuff all the time, and we decide if we want to keep it. That's his face in front of the church of the Salute. Isn't it wonderful?" Kit blinked.

"Oh, Trix, you mean you drew the Salute! Cool! It's very picturesque. We'll look at it later in your drawing book." Kit was silent the rest of the meal. She kept staring at the picture. She missed Ludovico.

4

On their second to last day in Venice, they all took the *vaporetto* together to go over to the *feria* in Campo San Polo. There were rides set up and food stalls with fried fish and sweet balls of fried dough and bleachers in front of a stage. Kit and her cousins rode the carousel. "Look, Trix, the horses of Saint Mark's," they laughed as they bobbed up and down. They all took seats together on the tier of benches as a band began to play opera tunes. Then the drummer started a stately beat and a costumed procession marched across the broad campo toward the stage. There were figures in masks and piebald colors, a tribute to Venetian *carnevale* traditions. There was a man dressed like a doge in an embroidered gown and a conical hat. There were men representing the garb of the old Venetian navy at the conquest of Constantinople and officials in modern Italian military uniforms. There was a man in carmine velvet with a large beard, possibly Titian or Aretino. There were women in straw hats with the crowns cut out to bleach their hair in the sun and the towering Venetian high heels, representing the overly social nuns of San Zaccaria, who entertained noble foreigners in their convent back in the day. Kit knew about all of this from her reading about the history of the city with her mother.

There were tributes to those two great modern Venetian institutions, the Film Festival and the Biennale. A couple were made up like '60s film stars, perhaps Marcelo Mastroanni and Sophia Loren; another guy was probably Fellini, with his own canvas director's chair. Then there were artists in paint-splattered smocks carrying palettes and brushes like they had been dragged out of their studios. Kit was the cheeriest she'd been in days watching the procession of colors file by.

Last in the menagerie was the mayor of Venice along with a handful of Venetians to be honored in a ceremony to present them with a medal signifying membership in the Order of St. Mark. One was an opera diva from the Fenice in a fancy gown. Another was a serious-looking scholar who had made great discoveries in the field of mathematics. The last was Ludovico.

Kit jumped up and let out a squeal. Her father laughed at her excitement. "Pretty cool, huh?" Ludovico spotted her as he was herded along, struggling with his cane. He raised it and winked at her. No one in the family noticed.

Seated on the stage, Ludovico sought her out with his eyes and smiled at her, his stately head encased in white hair bowing like a gentlemanly lion. When he received his award for lifetime achievement from the mayor, Kit felt her heart about to burst. Ludovico rose to give a speech. Kit made out that he said Maria couldn't be there, something about Treviso and her *"padre"* being taken *"inferma."* Ludovico looked wistful about his long career in the city, how he had to attend grade school under the Nazis, then grew to know Fellini and Stanley Kubrick, to travel the world, always to return to his old house in the city. But now, he said, it was time for a younger generation of artists. At this point, he called over an official and whispered something in her ear. Then turning back to the microphone, he said something about *"amica,"* then shifted to English and said, "I want to call up a representative of the new generation, my talented friend Kit."

Kit almost fell backward off her bleacher seat when Ludovico's finger pointed straight at her. The other eight members of her family were staring at her with sixteen huge dumbfounded eyes. A woman approached and led her away while the crowd applauded. When she reached the stage, Ludovico shook her hand politely and formally and announced to the crowd, "This is my friend Kit, the painter." The crowd erupted in cheers. Later, Kit couldn't really remember what had happened. She met the mayor, the opera singer, the famous mathematician. Then Ludovico invited the entire family across the canal to the Palazzo Grassi for a reception for the honorees. Her cousins, her parents, her grandparents, her aunt and uncle were almost speechless through the entire event as they watched Kit stand next to

Ludovico in the receiving line, shaking hands and smiling.

Ludovico took them all out to dinner that night at Ristorante Tiziano, at the same table sitting across from Kit's painting. He explained to her parents and grandparents that they had met when Kit escaped a rainstorm in his doorway, that his wife, Maria, had walked her back to their neighborhood, that Maria and he had gone to Treviso where her father was gravely ill, and that Kit was a fine artist. He also explained to Kit that he had arranged to sell her painting, but only if she wanted to, to the owner of Tiziano for 1,000 euros. Kit kind of wanted to take it home, but she and the family agreed that it would be cool to have it hanging there in Venice the next time they came, and she accepted a check from the owner.

After much merriment, good food, and wine, Kit's grandmother suddenly said, "Oh my god, we have to pack! We're leaving in the morning!" Kit embraced Ludovico and said she would see him "next time." He smiled and said, "You will."

The next evening, Kit sat in her room in Brooklyn staring at her sketchbook. "Papa," she said, "were we really in Venice yesterday?"

Her dad looked at her curiously and said, "I think so." She dumped her dirty clothes bag out on the floor and spotted the red socks.

"Yeah, I think we really were."

II

Kit's Roman Holiday

The sun was starting to set over Rome, and Kit measured the light outside on the orange sandstone of the balcony against the red tiles behind, then began her call to the post. "C'mon, everybody, we have to go to get there for the last rays of the sun!" Her parents, grandparents, aunt and uncle, and two cousins were sprawled around the room, rousing from a jet-lag nap to make up for losses on the overnight from New York. They'd just moved into their apartment in Trastevere a few hours before—and the other eight were sitting looking at Kit like a groggy army waiting to be led into battle. Her cousins Lily and Mia, her roommates, rubbed their eyes sleepily while the adults sipped some afternoon coffee from the espresso pot on the stove.

"You know what's just up the block from here? The church of St. Cecilia, patron saint of music, Papa!" Her father was a drummer.

"Are we going there now?" said her mom.

"No, later. St. Cecilia lived around 200 AD; they opened her grave about 1600, and her body hadn't decayed at all!"

"Really, like she looked just the same?" said Mia. "That's weird. Like 1400 years later?"

"They say her body was not corrupted."

"Corrupted? By what, like by vice or something."

"No, corrupted by death. And decay," Kit mused with a serious look on her face. "Well, that's what they say, but they also say they tried to kill her by striking her neck with a sword three times and she still lived for three days. So I don't know. About what they say."

"Did she play the guitar, like you?" inquired Lily.

"The drums!" said her aunt.

"No, she was forced to marry a rich guy, and she didn't want to, so during the wedding they say she was singing to God in her heart. That's why she's our patron saint. We musicians, I mean."

"Well, I know I'm always drumming to God when I play!" exclaimed her father, drumming his fingers on Kit's shoulder with a rat-a-tat-tat.

"Stop!"

Things had been going swimmingly well for Kit. Just as her fifth-grade class wound up their production of *The Odyssey* with her in the role of Pallas Athena, and were moving into the Rome unit, her granddad announced that the family trip this spring would be to Rome.

Her father had said, "Kit, at this moment at least, you probably know more about Rome than any of the rest of us." Accordingly, for the first night there, a Saturday, she marched them all down the street and across the first bridge over the river Tiber onto the Tiber island—"The end of the island is shaped like the prow of a ship," she tourguided—and over the second bridge into the Jewish Ghetto and around the huge ruins of the Teatro di Marcellus. Several tiers of dark ancient arches framed neatly cut gravestone-sized patches of blue sky in the dusk.

"That's incredible, KitKat," said her mom. "Where are you leading us?"

"You'll see, mama. You have to do this at sunset on your first night in Rome." They crossed the busy street beyond the theatre, where Kit pointed out the Tarpeian rock, sight of ancient executions, she extrapolated, and approached the Capitoline hill from behind. Kit skipped excitedly onto the broad scallops of the sweeping stairway that led up the hill and explained, "This is the Capitoline, one of the seven hills of ancient Rome. Michelangelo designed this stairway, but it wasn't built until after he died."

"See the women come and go, talking of Michelangelo," quipped her uncle, an English professor back in Brooklyn. To the left, the long flight of older stairs up to the primal church of the Aracoeli stretched up and away hundreds of steps in the darkening spring light. They reached the piazza at the top with the statue of Marcus Aurelius set in a perfectly calibrated middle spot with the shadows from the Capitoline museums cascading over them from the three sides opposite the stairway.

"This is thought to be one of the great public spaces in the world," announced Kit. "It really is the Renaissance, you know. But now, we have to go around the back of this building and you'll see what we came for." The troupe ambled around the building, Lily and Mia really leaping around with delight, and the adults following dutifully on.

"This is so cool, Kit!" effused Lily.

Off the terrace at the back of the Capitoline Hill, they looked down and across the Roman Forum, lit in the rose shades of the growing night and by a few artificial lights just coming on. There below was the Temple of Saturn, the Arch of Titus, the Temple of Vesta, the Palatine hill rising up off to the right, and the Colosseum in the distance. The entire family oohed and aahed except for Grandpa who didn't do such things. "Here on this spot," said Kit, "is where the Renaissance meets the ancient world." She paused for effect, and it worked. "And right now, at this moment, where the sun meets the moon."

Kit's grandmother let out a low gasp. "Kit, that is beautiful, so beautiful. Did you come up with that yourself?"

"I guess so," she said, shrugging. "I read about doing this, but I added the sun and the moon." This was a propitious beginning. The entire clan, awed by the experience curated by their youngest member, soaked up the moment.

"What was the Colosseum for?" said Lily.

"It was like a stadium," said Mia. "They had gladiator matches and wild animals ate the Christians."

"And people paid to see that?"

"Yeah, hundreds of thousands were murdered there."

"Doesn't Billy Joel play the Colosseum?" asked Lily.

"Yeah, he does," replied her sister.

"But I mean they wouldn't have, like Billy Joel at Dachau, would they?"

"No, I don't think so."

"What's the difference?"

"It's too recent. Maybe in a thousand years they'll have Billy Joel at Dachau."

"Girls!" said their grandmother.

"Well!" Mia frowned.

They all walked slowly back around the building and through the piazza and down the Capitoline steps with the magic mood of the evening suspended between them in silence. When they got to the bottom, the busy traffic on the Via del Teatro di Marcello broke the spell. "Here at the base of the Capitoline steps," said Kit, "is the spot where the marathon at the 1960 Rome Olympics began. It was won by the Ethiopian runner Abebe, who did the whole thing without shoes."

"Barefoot through the streets of Rome?" said her mom, a

runner herself.

“That’s right.” They proceeded back through the Ghetto, where Kit explained that the Jewish cuisine here dates from before the time of Christ.

After dinner at a local trattoria in Trastevere, recommended in the notes that came with their apartment, and a good night’s sleep dispensing with their jetlag once and for all, the next morning the entire family appealed to Kit to see what they should do next. “You’ve forgotten,” she said, “we have reservations at the Vatican!”

They gamely fought their way through the reservation protocol, the lines, the security checks to see the Sistine Chapel, the Pinacoteca, the Raphael Rooms, before joining the throngs at St. Peter’s.

While all agreed the sites were impressive, Lily summed up all of their feelings when she said, “I liked yesterday better. Kit’s tours are better!” In fact, the part they most enjoyed in the Vatican was when Kit explained all about the Laocoon: how to say it (lay-auck-un-a), how it was an ancient classical statue dug up by a guy in his backyard in the Renaissance, how Michelangelo went over to his house to take a look, and how it portrayed a serpent risen from the sea who is strangling Laocoon and his sons before they can warn the Trojans about the Greek guerrillas hiding inside the giant wooden horse that has been pulled inside the city walls of Troy.

“Wow, I didn’t know all that,” said Kit’s dad. Her uncle pointed out that Laocoon was later the name of a classic essay of German literature, by Goethe.

The third day, they had advance tickets to the Borghese Gallery in the Borghese Park overlooking the city. Here they saw the Bernini statue of *Apollo and Daphne*, where the beautiful woman in stone has half turned into a frozen tree, while her other half still runs from the sun god who has her in his clutches. "Does this come with a trigger warning?" said Kit's Aunt Jenna. They marveled at the five canvases by the great Baroque painter Caravaggio. After lunch, they moved back down the Corso to the site of their first-night stroll, the Capitoline and the museums there. Standing in their third major museum in twenty-four hours, Kit had an inspiration. They were looking at Caravaggio's painting of *The Fortune Teller*, where a young dandy is having his palm read by a young woman. "You guys want to have a scavenger hunt?!"

After all of their museuming, the family was ready for a little something different. Kit toyed with the idea of all of them re-creating the path of the medieval pilgrims and visiting the seven pilgrimage churches of Rome. But she was broadminded enough to understand that this would be a bit challenging, as St. Peter's was close; the Lateran, Santa Maria Maggiore, Santa Croce, and San Lorenzo fuori la mura were more or less in the same part of town; but San Giovanni fuori la mura and San Sebastiano were far away and walking the pilgrimage route would be what you must do if you were really going to play that game. "*Fuori la mura*" means "outside the wall," she explained. "You know, like the ramparts."

"The what?" said her dad.

"The ram-parts!"

"So here's the game," she said. "Caravaggio is the greatest Roman painter after Michelangelo and Raphael. We saw his *Deposition* in the Vatican, then more at the Borghese and *The Fortune Teller* here. You have to find as many other places in Rome with Caravaggios as you can visit and photograph on your cellphone." They all enthusiastically agreed and discussed the parameters of the rules. It was decided you could use everything: a guidebook and a map and your data, too. It would be hard enough to get around the city. They split up into four teams of two. Kit's uncle with his daughter Lily, Kit's mom Dani and her cousin Mia, her grandfather with her Aunt Jenna, and she and her dad.

The next morning after breakfast, the four teams set out while Grandma stayed home to prepare dinner and rest her legs. "Somehow, I think this game is rigged," said Kit's aunt. But all were seasoned competitors at something or other, and set out with their maps and books to track down the Caravaggios. Kit grabbed her dad by the arm and dragged him toward the tram that led over the Tiber into the center of town. When they got off the last tram stop by the site called the Argentina, Kit looked down into the full city block of ancient ruins lying 25 feet below the street level. "Look!" she said, pointing down. Across the expanse of slabs of fallen marble, stray cats lay lounging in the morning sun.

"How many can you count, Kit?" They got up to ten and thought that was it, and then they kept seeing new ones here and there and everywhere, camouflaged in their lassitude against the stone. When they hit thirty, Kit said they were losing time and had to go.

The family soon became cognizant of the fact that Kit had a keen sense of direction in the Imperial City. While none of them could really have been familiar with the grid of streets, she would say something like, "It's over there by the Pantheon," or "It's over toward the Colosseum," and invariably be right about the general direction.

"Come on!" said Kit, pulling her dad over a few blocks to the Gallery Doria Pamphili. It's a small museum with a reasonable admission price, so they anted up just to look for a Caravaggio. They found *The Flight Into Egypt* and Kit pulled out her phone. "It's not his greatest, but interesting, nonetheless," she said. She took a couple of pictures, but a man in a fancy suit stood in her way. "Probably one of the Senators playing hookey," she said, alluding to the institutions of government in the neighborhood. "This could get him in trouble!" she whispered, looking at a shot of the man in half of the frame with half of a Caravaggio in the other. But to be safe, she politely asked him in English if he would move. He shook out of whatever reverie he was having and moved aside while looking at her and not uttering a word. "Whatevs," she said.

While they were looking at the Caravaggio, they sensed a commotion down the far corridor of the L-shaped little museum. There were only a few people around in total, and they were now joined by a glamorous lady in a long blue dress with a committee of attendants around her. The group headed for the most celebrated painting in the collection, Velasquez's portrait of Pope Innocent V. Kit studied them: the lady in blue, a photographer, a couple of big guys, a museum official, and a nervous young woman with a clipboard and a cellphone. "Daddy, who is that!?"

"I don't know. Let's see if we can find out on the way out." They moved back down the corridor toward the Velasquez in its own little alcove room. The woman in blue and her entourage started walking directly toward them. The woman smiled at Kit in passing, and then the group parked in front of the Caravaggio.

The attendant at the front desk thought twice before telling them it was the Princess of Savoy, Princess Lianna. "Please don't tell anyone or I'll get in trouble!" confided the woman to Kit.

"One down!" she screamed as she hit the sidewalk. "Shall I text them yet?" she laughed.

"No, let's wait until we at least have two." Kit led her dad down the street past the Pantheon and toward the Piazza Navona. The next stop was the Church of Santa Maria de la Francese, or the French church. This one was free, but it helped if you had some eurochange to put in the machines that lit up the chapel where three Caravaggios hung on the walls. Just about every visitor in the church was off to the left in the back, crowded around the chapel. "Caravaggio painted these for this very church here in 1600 or so, and they have been here ever since," explained Kit. "This one on the left may be his masterpiece." Her father studied the wall, with the scene of a group of men around a table gambling or counting money. One dressed in finery toys with a stack of coins. A figure in the back behind another figure points to the money man; the figure's feet at the bottom are poised to turn and walk away. "It's *The Calling of*

Saint Matthew," said Kit, "Matthew, the tax collector. Jesus is the guy in the back and he's calling him to come with. People argue about whether Matthew is pointing at himself and saying, 'Who Me?' or pointing at the guy to his side, like 'Him?'" Her father commented how it was painted perfectly for the vantage point of the viewer standing right there in the church looking into the chapel, with light apparently streaming in from a window painted above the scene as if you were really looking at the group of men from the end of the room. Kit put her euro dimes in the machine and got a few shots on her iPhone.

As they were walking out, Kit hissed, "There's the princess coming in! She's doing the Caravaggio tour, too! Do you think she wants to play our game?" Kit thought the princess might have smiled at her as she walked by in the middle of her entourage. Kit reached for her phone to take a picture, but then stopped dead in her tracks and looked at a text. "Papa, we have to go, right now!" She ran out of the church, her baffled dad behind her. "We have to get a cab, we have to be there right now to get in."

"Who do you know to get a text from?"

"C'mon, Papa, hail a cab and I'll tell ya!" A cab pulled over, they hopped in, and Kit commanded, "Aurora 123, *pronto*!" She turned to her dad. "I called the concierge they gave us with the apartment and asked about this secret Caravaggio, which isn't open to the public. She just texted and said we could join a tour if we go right now!" The taxi crossed the Corso and worked its way up to the Via Veneto, taking the S curves by the Cappuchin church with the skulls that Kit said they would have to visit later and the American Embassy and then made a left at the top of the hill. They were dropped off in front of a large metal gate that led into an estate.

The gate was open and a bus was unloading people into the gravel road leading in. Noting that they were all adults and Italians, Kit implored her dad, "C'mon, act natural!" She grabbed his hand and rushed into the group, smiling and effusing *"Ciao!"* in one direction, bowing, then turning and beaming graciously to the other side, *"Ciao! Ciao!"* The Italian seniors looked at her in bafflement and smiled benignly. They thought she might be part of the entertainment. But soon, a guide was taking them all into the Casino d'Aurora, a summer cottage on the estate that belonged to a Caravaggio patron in the late 1500s. She showed them the mural on one ceiling of Mars and Apollo.

"Well I guess so," said Kit of the attribution. "It's not really like any of his classic work, could be by anybody really," she said. "But I'll take number three!" She shot a few photos. Then as the group moved into the following room with the lecture in Italian continuing, Kit pressed a hand on her father's forearm, smiled and nodded all around, and gently let the crowd sift forward around them as they drifted back and back further and then backed out the door into the sunlight. "Yes! Score!" Kit exulted as she skipped down the lane.

A few raindrops began to fall. Kit said aloud: "Roman rain, stony lane, Roman lane, rites of spring. Mmmm." She couldn't quite finish her verse. They moved around the corner and back into the Borghese Park where they'd visited the Borghese Gallery. "So is up here one of the seven hills of Rome?" her father asked.

"No," said Kit. We're up on the Pincio, a famous walk up here over the city, but it's not one of the hills. Neither is the Gianicolo, the big one over us in Trastevere next to the Vatican. The seven are over there: the Capitoline, the Viminal, the Quirinal, the Caelian ("the Cheeelian," she elongated), the Esquinale, the Aventine, the Palatine," she recited. It started to pour harder. "We can go right down into the Popolo," she said. They carefully stepped down a long wet set of stone stairs and landed right next to the side door of the church of Santa Maria del Popolo, facing out into the wide circular plaza with the same name, with the campanile in the middle and the pair of matching churches flanking the Corso, leading in on the other side. Here, they saw the two Caravaggio masterpieces. Kit asked the priest if he had seen the princess today. He nodded inconclusively and smiled down at her.

When the rain quit, they made their way down to San Agostino where Kit explained that the Virgin in the Caravaggio there was modeled after a prostitute and that she's stepping on a snake. "Like she's a protector." They exited and Kit texted her cousins with a taunt about the number 5. She led the way over to the Barberini Gallery, just below the Via Veneto. They had really just made a loop up to the Casino d'Aurora, down to the Popolo, to San Agostino close to the Francese, and now back to the west a few blocks. When they entered the wide drive to the museum, a black SUV swept by. The princess got out and entered the Barberini. "C'mon," said Kit. "We know she's going straight to the Caravaggios."

Kit and her dad beat the royal crew to the collection of Caravaggios. Kit stopped in front of the one of Judith beheading Holofernes and stared, confounded. Her dad was absorbed in the painting, too. "I guess it would be like that," Kit stammered.

"Yeah, I guess so."

"You know, the guy getting beheaded is Caravaggio."

"What do you mean?"

"It's a self-portrait. I wonder why he did that. Do you think he thought he deserved it somehow? It's pretty gruesome for a joke." An old woman in the painting standing next to Judith holds a sack for the head.

"Well… back to my silly game!" she joked brittlely, aware of all the ironies, mocking herself with a degree of sophistication beyond her years.

After getting her photos, they descended through the small museum when Kit looked to her left into a gallery and quickly turned away. The man who'd blocked her view at the Doria Pamphili was considering Raphael's famous portrait of his mistress, *La Fornarina*. The man didn't see Kit. She shivered and plowed forward with her dad. "Kit, I have to run in the restroom," he said.

"OK." She was anxious to move on to the next Caravaggio. She waited for her dad just inside the entrance to the museum. She stood looking out the door down the cobbled lane that slopes through a wall and some trees up to the palazzo. A taxi came up the entranceway and two men in dark blue suits got out and looked at their cellphones. The driver idled and the men didn't pay their fare. Kit walked out the door into the sunshine and approached the car. "Hey, can we have that car?" she asked the two men, planning their next stop over across the Tiber at the Corsini Gallery. They looked at her in seeming disbelief, apparently not understanding English. One shook his head emphatically, while the other gestured at the driver.

The taxi driver looked at her fixedly and said, "No, no, pickup, pickup!" Kit shrugged and walked back over and reentered the museum. She took a couple of steps into the gift shop and spun the postcard rack. She selected the Raphael and two Caravaggios and then saw one of the architect Borromini's spiral ramp in some part of the Barberini palazzo, which hadn't been open when they were upstairs. Just then, she saw the princess and her party come out of the elevator on their way out. Kit put down the postcards and pulled out her phone.

She stood in the entranceway and tried to fade into the background (like Robert Frank shooting *The Americans*, she thought), acting like she was checking her messages, but surreptitiously snapping a couple of shots just when the princess passed her on the threshold. She held the camera down at her waist and snapped off a couple more of the group.

The Caravaggio-blocker guy from the Doria Pamphili followed them out the door and she had an inkling that he was something like Italian secret service, advancing the princess's visits to the museums and protecting her from afar. A black SUV had pulled into the front area and the entourage headed toward it.

Later, Kit would try to put together exactly the order of the next few seconds. The two men from the taxi suddenly leapt forward and swung their fists viciously into the faces of the bodyguards on either side of the princess, sending them both sprawling on the ground. The man she had thought was a protector lunged at the woman handler and pushed her to the pavement, sending a clipboard and a high heel bounding across the stones. The woman gasped, as the man grabbed the princess with his hand over her mouth and moved into the back of the cab with her in his violent grasp. One man got in the back on the other side and the third jumped into the shotgun seat. As he got in, he yelled, *"Allahu Akbar!"* Kit wasn't quite sure, but she thought it was a very Italian Allahu Akbar. A museum guard in a uniform motioned at them with a truncheon, but held back as he didn't seem to have a gun.

Without thinking, Kit ran out into the sun with her phone and started shooting pictures of the taxi. She deftly shot the license plate and looked for a number in the window. Through the back window, she saw the princess's terrified eyes with a hand over her mouth. Kit's eyes locked on the eyes of the guy who'd been shadowing her and the princess in multiple museums. She shuddered at the look of cutthroat hate in his eyes, as he fixed on her, with the car squealing its tires and speeding down the cobbled lane. It seemed so weird, this peaceful, isolated little piazza at the entrance to this museum suddenly transformed into a crime scene.

The two bodyguards had roused themselves from the ground; one gingerly rubbed his jaw while the other helped the woman up and handed her the missing high heel. The museum guard was frantically on the phone shouting in Italian. Sirens were heard nearby within a minute.

Kit's dad emerged from the museum. "What's next, KitKat?" he said cheerfully, not really able to take in all that had happened in the previous two minutes.

"We've got to go now!" said Kit.

"Where's the next stop, the next Caravaggio?" he said.

"Forget Caravaggio, we've got to go to the police. Now!" she said. But right then, a Carabinieri car with flashing lights sped into the courtyard, and three men jumped out.

"What happened?" stammered her father.

"They kidnapped the princess."

"What? You saw it?"

"Yeah. I need to talk to the police." The three policemen were frantically talking to the guard and shouting into their phones and the police radio in their car. Two more police cars sped in to join them. Kit's dad approached the trio.

"Excuse me, *signori*," he started.

"No, no," said one of the policemen, waving him off. "No time! No time!" The guard was talking to them, and Kit heard him use the words, "Allahu Akbar," and "ISIS."

"But officer," said her father.

"Sir, a crime has taken place here. We cannot help you."

"But..."

"Did you witness the crime, sir?"

"No, but my daughter was standing over there when it happened."

"Sir, a child will not be helpful to this investigation!" Kit stood with her arms crossed, her phone in one hand resting under her opposite arm. She smirked.

"C'mon papa, they're not going to listen to me." Kit paused and walked back into the museum. She addressed a woman behind the counter. "Excuse me, could you tell me where the office of the *carabinieri* is?" At this point, police officers were mounting the steps of the museum and taking what seemed to Kit useless pictures all over the place. The woman, shaken by the recent events, wrote down the address for Kit on the back of a Caravaggio postcard. "C'mon, Papa, let's go, time is of the essence." They walked through the courtyard and out on to the Via delle Quattro Fontane. "We have to get a taxi. Do you have some money?"

"Kit, where are we going?"

"To the police station, Papa. They will want to talk to me there." It was just a few blocks away.

"Damn, Kit, what did you see?"

"I'll tell you in just a minute!" The taxi pulled up at the *carabinieri* station and they ran up the steps to the front desk.

"Let me talk," Kit said. Her father gave her a look. At the front reception desk no one was paying attention to them. Kit announced loudly, "We have some information regarding the kidnapping of Princess Lianna! Let us see a detective. Time is of the essence." The bored, inattentive officer there perked up at this little girl.

"How did you know about this? It just happened."

"I was there," said Kit. "Let me talk to a detective." The man grabbed the phone and talked animatedly with his eyes on Kit. A man in a suit and a woman emerged from the back and ushered her and her Dad through a door into an office.

"Hello, I am Inspector Giovanelli and this is Inspector Napoletano. Who are you?"

"My name is Kit Maxwell, and I was standing at the entrance to the Barberini palace when they kidnapped Princess Lianna."

"We have reason to think it was ISIS that did it," said the woman.

"I don't think so," said Kit. They stared at her wide-eyed. They turned toward her father.

"Were you there, Mr. uh Mix-well?"

"Uh, no, I was in the bathroom at that particular time." They turned back to Kit.

"And why is it you think it wasn't ISIS, Signorina?" asked

Inspector Giovanelli.

"Well, you know a lot more about this than I do," Kit said slyly, "but does ISIS usually commit their terrorist acts in really really nice suits? I mean maybe they do. It would be a good disguise, but on the news I always see them dressed as workers or something like that. Besides, I mean I don't really know how this works, but if it was ISIS, wouldn't they have shot the bodyguards and the museum guy and me, too, I mean if it was really ISIS committing a terrorist act. Besides, I know there are a lot of Muslims in this country, but when he yelled 'Allahu Akbar' it sounded pretty Italian to me." The inspectors looked at each other with their heads moving backwards and then turned back to Kit like robotic honing sensors.

"I have some pictures here," she said. "First of all, this is the license plate number that was on the taxi." Inspector Napoletano leaned in and wrote the number on a pad. She picked up the phone and shouted out the numbers in Italian. "Then here are the men getting into the cab. And here's a picture of the princess and the guy in the back as they were getting away." Inspector Giovanelli looked with interest at her screen.

"This is very helpful, Signorina. But we can't quite make out the guy in the back."

"Oh I have another picture of him," Kit said.

"What?"

"Earlier today, we were over at the Doria Pamphili, and the princess was there, and that guy was there, too."

"What? You have another picture of the same man over there?"

"Yes, I have come to the conclusion that he was following her, from one museum to the other. See we were playing this game where we were tracking down all the Caravaggios in Rome, so we were at the Doria Pamphili this morning and the princess was doing the same thing, not as thorough of course, but we saw her over at *The Calling of Saint Matthew* in the Francese. That man wasn't there, and then we went to the Casino Nobile and the Popolo before San Agostin and then we got to the Barberini. And then I saw that man in there before the princess arrived." Kit offered the picture of the Caravaggio-blocker getting in the way of *The Flight Into Egypt*.

"My god," said Giovanelli. "We know this man. He's Cosa Nostra, not ISIS." The phone rang and Inspector Napoletano picked it up.

"The license plate was a fake," she said. "It doesn't exist."

"But we know where these people go," said Giovanelli. He dialed a number and gave rapid-fire instructions into the phone. He grabbed his coat and turned to Kit. "I need to take your phone!" he shouted, "as evidence." Kit scrunched up her nose and looked at her dad.

"Well there goes the Caravaggio game," she sighed, exasperated, all her hard work going down the drain for a little kidnapping and correcting the ineptitude of the *carabinieri*. "Well, we all do have civic responsibilities. You going to give it back?" she shouted after the inspectors as they raced out of the room.

"Yes, leave your name!" said Napoletano as she raced away. Kit and her dad left their names with the guard at the front desk. Kit wrote down her phone number and then crossed it out.

"Oh yeah, they have my phone. You better write yours down. Come to think of it, they can't get into my phone without my fingerprint. If only I had texted or emailed you the Caravaggio pictures, we'd still be in the game! Oh well." They walked somewhat despondently over to the Campo Fiori and got some white pizza at the Antico Forno bakery. They sat on the fountain in the square and ate their slices.

"You know what, KitKat? For one thing, we are still on vacation in Rome, and that isn't a bad thing. Secondly, you did the right thing and you might have really helped the police. So we should celebrate."

"Yeah, I know." They walked over and caught the tram back across the Tiber to Trastevere to meet the rest of the family for the scheduled 4 o'clock end to the Carravaggio game. The other teams did well, but not quite as well as Kit would have if she still had her phone.

"That was a great game, Kit! Thank you for making that up. It really got us out and around Rome, and seeing the Caravaggios was amazing. What happened to your phone? Did you drop it into the Tiber?"

Kit smiled and said, "Well, we were in a museum where there was a crime, and the police wanted to check out a picture of mine." She was too tired to explain the whole thing. She lay down to take a nap before they cooked dinner.

When she woke up, her father told her that Inspector Giovanelli had called. He was coming by the apartment to bring back her phone. "Really?" she said. "Will my Caravaggios still count?"

"Well, your cousin had the pictures here at 4 o'clock, so she wins. But hey, it was for extra dessert at dinner, so I think you can live with that." They were sitting around having a melon and an olive oil cake for dessert when the buzzer rang. Inspectors Giovanelli and Napoletano came up the stairs and were introduced around the room to the family.

The pair cornered Kit's mother and grandparents and Napolitano asked, "Do you know what your child did today?" They said that they were waiting for her to tell the whole story. "She very probably saved the life of Lianna, Princess of Savoy, who was kidnapped today by the mafia. We need you all to keep this quiet. We would have put Kit on the cover of all the newspapers tomorrow, but that might endanger all of your lives, both here in Rome or even in America. They had planned to broker a ransom for her and tried to act like it was ISIS doing the crime, but it was Kit and her picture that tipped us off to the Cosa Nostra. With that clue, we knew where to look and have arrested the four men involved. They will be put away for a long time, but the mafia, is, unfortunately, always around."

"Well, my daughter was happy to help," said Kit's dad. "But you interrupted our visit to the Caravaggio trail."

"Ah yes," said Giovanelli. "We love our Caravaggios! But you know, he was a criminal, too!"

"But a groundbreaking artist," said Kit. "He started Baroque painting." Everyone looked at her.

"The princess is resting tonight after her ordeal today," said Napoletano. "But she wants to send her profound thanks. We told her what you did."

"Tell her highness you're welcome," said Kit. The next day, Kit's dad's phone rang, and this time it was the princess on the other end of the line.

"Kit, you saved my life!" she said. "I so wish I could bring you to my house and meet you, but the police think it would be dangerous. I'm talking on a disguised phone line so they can't trace it. I think I'll just have to meet you in New York!"

"No problem, Princess," said Kit. "Just come on out to Brooklyn."

A few weeks later, Kit received a box at her Brooklyn home. It came from a jeweler and had a card without too much identification. It said, *"Mille grazie!"* and was signed "PL." Inside was a brooch, which Kit discovered represented the coat of arms of the House of Savoy. Kit's dad thought it was made of valuable jewels. Her mom said it might pay for her college education. But Kit insisted on pinning it on the belt line of her jeans. Her parents said they needed to get an appraisal, but Kit said then she wouldn't really feel comfortable wearing it around, and it was hers, and she wanted to enjoy it, and everyone would think it was "costume jewelry from the Brooklyn Flea anyway."

Five years later, a bestseller was published in Italy. Translated, the title was *The Little Girl Who Saved a Princess*. It was written by a former policeman who had quit to become a writer. He used a pseudonym for discretionary purposes, as he had worked on many cases involving the mafia. All the names had been changed to protect the innocent.

III

Paris: The Princess and the Snail

At dinner on their first night, Kit announced her priorities for the week in Paris. She said they were, more or less in this order: first and foremost, French cuisine, then the fashion scene, followed by art and architecture, and finally literature.

Her uncle John, the English professor, said he'd have her covered on the literature part. He gave her an illustrated copy of *The Little Prince* by Antoine de Saint-Exupéry, knowing that she would appreciate the space connection, and the fact that the author was a pilot. And he promised to school her all about the great French writers.

His wife, Jenna, reeled off their museum destinations: the Louvre, the Pompidou, the Jeu de Paume, the Musée d'Orsay, and the Jacquemart, plus the Eifel Tower and at least Notre Dame and the Sacre Coeur. They hoped to have time to see the cathedral at St. Denis. "And then we have to walk around all the arrondissements and see the neighborhoods, not just the sixth," she said, referring to their apartment on the Rue Dupuytren on the Left Bank.

Her mother said they had to go to the massive Les Puces flea market at Porte de Clignancourt and that, on the fashion front, she had scheduled a lesson in making hats for Kit and her two cousins.

Kit, now 11, turned to study the menu in the brasserie. Beautiful shades of amber light reflected off gleaming metal and colored glasswork in vegetal forms throughout the room. "This place is gorgeous!" said Kit. "I want to learn about French food."

"What's good?" deadpanned her father.

"Well I know I like French bread!" said Kit. "I love Italian food, but the bread's even better here."

"OK, *mon petite baguette*!" he said, poking her in the stomach with his finger. "What about the escargots," said her father, pronouncing the hard "t."

"It's S-CAR-GO, Papá," said Kit, putting a little French zest on the second syllable of Papá. "They're snails!"

"Can we eat those, I mean, as pescatarians?" asked her uncle.

"What's a pescatarian?" said Kit's grandmother.

"It's somebody who doesn't eat meat but eats fish," explained her uncle. "But where do snails fit in to that?"

"Is it like a fish? Are there sea snails?" asked his daughter Mia.

"Ooooh!" said her sister Lily.

"I'm not sure," their father mused. "I'm not sure, but I don't think so. But it wouldn't be like eating a warm-blooded mammal, or eating a bird with wings. And it has a shell, doesn't it? So it's kind of like a lobster or a shrimp. I think I'm gonna order them."

"Or maybe like a bug!"

"Dad's gonna eat snails!"

"S-CAR-GO!" said Kit.

"See the women come and go, talking of S-CAR-GO!" said Mia, almost shouting. Lily and Kit cracked up, while Kit's uncle looked on appreciatively for their remembering his T. S. Eliot quote from Rome the previous year.

"See the Maxwells come and go, eating their S-CAR-GO!" said Lily.

"See the *chefs de cuisine* come and go, braising their escargot!" howled Kit. The three of them doubled over with laughter.

"See the woman come and go, walking her escargot!" said Mia. "Her pet escargot!"

"Girls!" said Kit's Aunt Jenna. "Get a grip."

"Yes," said Kit. "We are in Paris and we need to act proper. Close your mouth when you chew, Papá, you are in Paris now. *Bien sur.*" Kit sat up in her chair, her back straight as a pine tree, and stuck her nose in the air. "We have to show some class."

"Well you are full of sass," said her father.

"Don't be crass," said Lily.

"You're a real literal lass," said her dad.

"Don't act like trash," said Mia.

"We musn't be *déclassé, Madam-moiselles!*" said Kit, waving at her cousins with her napkin.

"*Madam-moiselle*-Maxwell," said her dad.

"Lily and Mia come and go, while John eats his S-CAR-GO!" said Kit, and she and her two cousins broke out in laughter again. The adults rolled their eyes.

Only John and Kit's grandfather ended up eating the snails. They agreed they were "pretty good" but wouldn't promise to order them again. Lily picked up two empty escargot shells and moved them across the tablecloth. "Hello, Kit, we are your pet escargots, would you like to pet us?"

"Nooooo," Kit howled. She opted for the French onion soup, some *pommes frites* with mayonnaise, *une salade*, and a *crème brulee*. "That was sooooo good," she said. "Papá, we have to make *crème brulee*."

"Sure, we can do that."

"And we must see some Delacroix," said Kit. The other eight of them stared at her.

"You know, the Romantic painter… of many battle scenes…. And we simply must visit some of the *grand magasins*," she said with a flourish.

"What's that?" asked Lily.

"They're the classic department stores of Paris. Kind of like Bloomingdale's, but better."

Over his little cup of coffee *serré*, her uncle said, "Kit, I have a story about a French woman that I think you might like: 'A Simple Heart' by Gustave Flaubert. He was one of the greatest of all French writers. He would sit at his desk for twelve hours a day, and he was such a perfectionist, he might only come up with one sentence."

"One sentence! In twelve hours?" Kit said, incredulous, as she was known for a high-octane output of words per minute.

"Yes, but it would be a perfect sentence. Perhaps one of the finest sentences ever written in the history of literature. He made sure it was good. He is a good example of making sure that whatever you do, you do well."

"How many books did he write, at the rate of one sentence a day?"

"Well, some days he wrote more than that, but he didn't put out that many books. *Madame Bovary* is one of the greatest novels every written. But you'll have to wait to read that until you are an adult."

"Why?"

"It's about a bored housewife, and you haven't really reached a point where you ever get bored! And then there's *The Sentimental Education*. You really have to be old to understand that book. But I think you would enjoy 'A Simple Heart.' It's about a woman who thinks her parrot is God."

"Her parrot is God? That would make you a pescatarian for reals," said Kit.

"Now, other ways of writing can work, too. Balzac was a French writer here in Paris. And he wrote over 100 books. It was said that he drank over fifty cups of coffee a day."

"Fifty cups of coffee!"

"Yes. You see you can write in different ways. Flaubert was a perfectionist, while Balzac tapped into the flow of Paris, and spent all of his time writing about practically everybody and everything around him."

Kit was quickly getting into the rhythm of checking off all of her Paris boxes. She thanked John for the perspective on French literature. She had so much to do!

Her interest in checking out the Paris fashion scene came from her role as a fashionista at her elementary school. But she wasn't all about having the latest, most expensive clothes with a trendy label. She was much more about setting trends herself, in being a fashion icon, more McQueen than Fendi or Gucci. When she was 5, her mother asked what she wanted to be for Halloween, and Kit declared, "A nut box."

"A what?"

"A nut box."

"You mean like a box that holds nuts?"

"A nut box!" she insisted. So they had constructed one for her and she went out trick-or-treating in a nut box, setting herself off as a maverick among the witches and ghosts of her neighborhood.

On their first full day in Paris, Kit's mom took the three girls and her sister-in-law to the hat shop. They introduced themselves to Madame Lescaux, a sophisticated-looking older French lady who taught a workshop where kids could fashion their own headgear. What kind of chapeau would Kit like to construct? "Would you like a beret?" she asked.

"A cloque," said Kit. The madame showed them a number of possible fabrics; Mia and Lily chose red and black velvet and decided to make cloques, too. They cut pieces into long shapes, then learned how to close the seams and attach the pieces together. Soon they had lovely caps enveloping their scalps with their hair peeping out and cascading down to their shoulders. But Kit asked if there were any prints. There was a room full of different patterns in the hat shop and she carefully surveyed the wall. Finally, she found what she wanted, a shell pattern, perhaps of the inside of a nautilus. "The house of S-CAR-GO," said Kit, and the teacher laughed uncertainly.

They fashioned a cloque using the material. When they were close to being finished, Kit intervened and added two details. Two wisps of wire covered in velvet were added to stick out like antennae, while two glass buttons on either side evoked snail eyes. It wasn't a literal representation. "The print of the hat shows the inside of the snail's house," said Kit, "and these things are his eyes and ears, like he's looking back at you looking into his house." The teacher looked back at her, raising an eyebrow.

"Well, yes, yes, that's interesting, that's quite interesting, that's actually, actually quite clever the way you've come at the subject with different indications of the snail. It's actually quite brilliant. I think you have a future as a hatmaker." Lily and Mia agreed.

"Our hats are beautiful, Kit," said Mia, "but yours is so original. Will you be our little cousin snail?"

"Escargot!" said Kit. The teacher let out a full-throated laugh and then looked overcome, like she was going to cry, she was so amused.

"Your children are really extraordinary," she said to Kit's mom.

"Oh, only one of them is mine," she said vaguely, without explaining.

"I really think that snail hat is something," said the hatmaker. "Say, will you come back this week and let me copy it? I think I'd like to make another." They agreed, said they would give it a test run on the streets of Paris, and would come back. They all thanked her, and each girl dramatically gave her a kiss successively on both cheeks.

"Merci, beaucoup!" said Lily, and they all left, elated with their new creations.

"Mamá!" said Kit, in her new French accent, "there's something I want to make to go with this. Can you buy me a T-shirt to

paint on?"

"Is that something you want to do when we get back to Brooklyn next week?"

"No, no, I have to do it now to wear here in Paris, with my hat. You'll see." Her mother agreed and they bought a simple white T-shirt. Back at their apartment Kit got out her paint box, which she always brought wherever she went. She considered the palette of the blank front of the T-shirt.

"Are you going to paint a snail?" said Mia. "I mean an S-CAR-GO."

"Mmmmmm. No, I think I want to do a rebus," said Kit.

"Like a puzzle?"

"Sort of. *Papá, s'il vous plait*, what is a kind of French car?"

"What do you mean? Like a brand of car?"

"Yeah, like that."

"Well, a really common one is the Renault, it's kind of like the Ford of France. Lots of people have them."

"Can you show me a picture?" Her father searched on his laptop and soon came up with a range of Renaults, different models from different eras. "Cool," said Kit. "I think I like that best," she said as she made a sketch of it. "So, Papá, in France on a stoplight, is the green light on the top or the bottom?"

“I don’t know.”

“Oh, that’s OK, it doesn’t really matter, if it’s wrong, it will give it a nice American slangy kind of feel; they might like that in France. They don’t use the word ‘car’ anyway, but rather ‘auto,’ but I think they’ll get the idea.”

“What are you talking about?”

“You’ll see in a few minutes.” Kit drew a tall “S” on the left side of the front of her T-shirt and painted it over in blue. Next to it she sketched in the form of the Renault and painted that in red. Then on the right side she painted a stoplight with the top circle in green.

“Look *Papá*,” she said. He stared, baffled. Lily came into the room and looked at the shirt.

“Oh, cool, it’s a puzzle! I’ve got it! It’s S-AUTO-LIGHT! SAUTO-LIGHT! Satellite! Satellite! I know how much you like space!”

“No, that’s not it at all,” said Kit.

“No,” screamed Mia, “it’s S-CAR-GO! Escargot! I get it! I get it!”

“That’s hilarious,” said Kit’s dad, in a very serious tone.

“Oh, I see,” said Lily sheepishly. “Well, maybe it has a double meaning as a satellite.”

"Yeah, I like that," said Kit. "Fashion always can use another layer of meaning."

"It's snail fashion! Like snail mail!" said Mia.

They all took an afternoon walk from their apartment on the Left Bank across the river Seine to the Louvre. Kit wore what would come to be known as her snail hat and the escargot T-shirt. Lily convinced Mia to dress up in the long silver dress she had brought to attend the opera so that she looked like a princess, while Lily herself wore a chic pinstriped suit. "I am a fashion photographer," she declared, grabbing her camera. "And I am shooting the princess and her escargot for French *Vogue*! See the Princess of Maxwell come and go, strolling with her escargot!"

On the way to the museum, the three of them attracted lots of notice, Mia for her dress and Kit for her escargot getup and Lily for the professional demeanor she brought to the task of photographing the other two. A few people actually asked Lily what they were doing and she explained grandiloquently, "She is the Princess of Maxwell accompanied by her escargot." She kept a straight face with an exaggerated sense of self-importance as she said this.

In the tree-lined esplanade outside the Louvre, her uncle John took Kit by the hand and said, "KitKat, here's another line from T. S. Eliot." He reached up and put his palm toward the spring leaves on the trees above them. "Let us go then, you and I, and touch the leaves against the sky."

"That's cool, John." Later in the week, she would remind him of this moment and read him a quote she found from Coco Chanel: "I consider lace to be one of the prettiest imitations ever made of the fantasy of nature; lace always evokes for me those incomparable designs which the branches and leaves of trees embroider across the sky, and I do not think that any invention of the human spirit could have a more graceful or precise origin."

"That's lovely, Kit, and you have it right, that does feel like the line from T. S. Eliot. But you are imitating nature in your clothes in your own way."

They all went into the Louvre, and after the *Mona Lisa*, the things Kit really wanted to see were the paintings by Delacroix and then, of course, *The Death of the Virgin* by Caravaggio.

T. S. Eliot had stuck with the girls. "See the women come and go, looking for Caravaggio!" said Lily. They walked down the long corridor and found the painting in the long, long line of masterpieces and stood in front of it, considering the scene. The Virgin Mary was laid out on a slab of marble in a red dress.

"Wow, that's intense," said Kit's dad. "I thought the Virgin Mary didn't die, like didn't she go up to Heaven in the Assumption?"

"How should I know?" said his brother-in-law. "I'm Jewish. And non-scriptural at that." He paused. "But I guess she had to die first. That is sad. I don't really remember seeing that scene painted before. He is a great painter."

"See the girl with the red dress on," said Kit's dad. "She won't be dancin' all night long."

Lily photographed the princess and her escargot in front of the *Venus de Milo* and then in front of the *Winged Victory*. The trio attracted the attention of lots of passersby and then a tour group. The guide from the Louvre explained to the group in English, "Here at the Louvre, we are often privileged to be the setting for photo shoots for the fashion industry. It is rather a perfect synergy, the beauty of the Louvre as the perfect backdrop for fashion." She turned to the girls. "Ah that outfit is so clever! What is it you're shooting for?"

"It's the Princess of Maxwell and her friend, the escargot, and we are shooting for French *Vogue*," announced Lily, well practiced now in her ruse.

"Ah, yes, yes, French *Vogue*, how wonderful! That is a very clever outfit. Wonderful!" Kit and Mia struck a pose, Mia as a sophisticated French fashion model, Kit as, well, sort of a snail. Lily dipped and danced around them, shooting various angles with the drama she imagined involved in a fashion shoot. The tour group oohed and aahed and broke into a polite French-museum-appropriate applause. Several people walking by asked if they could take their picture. Some of them had some serious-looking cameras.

As all of this was going on, Kit's mom and dad, her grandmother and grandfather, and her aunt and uncle all stood by, dumbfounded, shaking their heads, smiling. At one point, Kit's dad couldn't stand it any longer and, turning his head away from the scene, let out a loud guffaw. Kit's grandmother whispered to her husband, "God bless the child that's got her own will!" and started laughing.

The party left the Louvre and walked down to the Place des Vosges in the Marais. As they moved, Kit kept them apprised of when they had moved from the first to the second and then the third arrondissement. "The Place des Vosges is both in the third and the fourth arrondissement, sitting on the border," she informed them like a tour guide. There in the arcaded quadrant surrounding the grass of the square, they were all amused to find a "real" fashion shoot going on, with lighting technicians and harried assistants giving directions and willowy models in expensive-looking clothes.

Kit walked by the shoot in her escargot hat and T-shirt, with Mia trailing behind and Lily snapping pictures of both. The fashion photographer held her camera down at her waist and eyed Kit. Momentarily, she forgot the array of fashion professionals before her and considered Kit's hat. She looked curiously at it and then at Lily and Mia. Lily bowed down almost to the ground in a sweeping gesture, and solemnly intoned, like she was announcing the guests at a grand ball, "The Princess of Maxwell and her escargot." The fashion photographer bowed back graciously in a formal curtsey.

"*Mademoiselles,*" she said, "might I have the privilege of taking your picture?"

"Why certainly, *Madame,*" said Lily, "it would be a great honor for the princess and her escargot." The woman kneeled and shot all three of them from several angles. A show runner on that other fashion shoot looked exasperated. The models broke character. One lit a cigarette.

"Where on earth did you get that outfit, *Mademoiselle*

Escargot?" asked the photographer.

"This old thing?" said Kit. "I made it." Kit shrugged and rolled her eyes.

Later, over dinner, the entire crew of nine couldn't get over their afternoon. They kept laughing, howling, shrieking. Even the grandparents couldn't stop laughing over the adolescent ruse factor. "See the models come and go, wishing they were escargot!" said Lily.

"Congratulations on your shoot, *Madame*!" said Kit to Lily.

"Say, could you have the servants bring me another Perrier?" said the princess.

The group talked about their plans for the next day. Kit's mom had always wanted to see the little Jacquemart museum.

"Le Jacquemarrrrrt," said Kit, rolling her r like in "Montmartre." "Is that Jacques's Mart? Do they have hot dogs and slurpees there?" she asked.

"Le Kwik Marrrrrt!" said Lily, rolling the r.

"Le Seven Eleven!" said Mia.

"You gals are really silly," said Kit's mom.

"Je regret, Mamá," said Kit, with a strong accent on the last syllable, and a healthy dose of mock sincerity.

The three agreed they had to wear the same clothes at least for one more day. Later it would be commented on how the escargot girl appeared at the Louvre and the Place des Vosges and then the next day at the Jacquemart and then the Eiffel Tower.

They took fashion shots from the top of the latter, looking over the city while Kit pointed her antennae at various famous monuments across the skyline: the Arc de Triomphe, Les Invalides, Notre Dame, Le Sacre Coeur.

That evening, they went out to eat at the Café Flor on the Boulevard Saint-Germaine, near where they were staying. When they entered, the maître d' greeted them enthusiastically. "Yes, yes, please come in, we have your table for nine ready." They did not order any escargots this time, but kept the good spirits going. They really felt like they were having such a good time that everyone else in the bistro was watching them with jealousy of their high dudgeon.

"We're not being too loud, are we?" said Kit's grandmother.

"I don't think so," said her husband. "We're just the toast of Paris, you know." At the end of their meal, the waiter brought over a dessert cart and gave them an assortment of complimentary desserts.

The maître d' returned. "Was everything very good, here?" he said. "Very good, very good," he said nervously, not waiting for an answer. But they all eagerly agreed that the meal was indeed very good. "It is a privilege to have you here. We so enjoyed you on the cover of *Le Monde*!"

"Haha, that is very funny!" said Kit's mom.

"I have a copy. Would you autograph it for me?" said the maître d' to Kit.

"Haha," said Kit. "Of course, I will be happy to sign autographs at any time." The maître d' left for a moment and came back with the day's newspaper in his hand.

He laid it down on the table in front of Kit. For the first time in at least 48 hours, the entire Maxwell clan was silent. They looked on, speechless, at the cover of *Le Monde* with Mia mugging for the camera in her long silver dress, Kit waxing buglike at her side, and Lily kneeling and framing them in a square made by her hands. They were pictured in the Place des Vosges.

"W-T-H?" Kit's mom said in code. John, who could read French, perused the paper.

He read, "The mysterious escargot girl was seen at the Louvre and the Place des Vosges with an unidentified princess." The nine of them sat frozen; there was a long, long pause. It lasted for some time. They all searched one another's faces with puzzled serious expressions like they had just discovered King Tut's tomb and were trying to think of what to say about it.

Lily finally broke the silence: "Unidentified? She's the Princess of Maxwell!" Then everyone broke out laughing. Kit and Lily and Mia signed the *Le Monde* for the maître d' and then they asked him if they could still get copies and he directed them to the newsstand down at the corner of the Rue Bonaparte.

They were all exhilarated by the fifteen minutes of fame and their featuring on the tabloid press in Paris. "Like Page Six of the *New York Post*," said Kit's grandma. But they really really were not prepared when Kit appeared on the cover of *Le Monde* again on the following day with a picture from the Eifel Tower and a report that they had been spotted at the Jacquemart museum.

By the end of the week before their vacation was over, a major avant-garde fashion designer had announced that he was inspired to incorporate into his fall line an escargot pattern inspired by the little girl's hat. A fashion critic formulated that the hat's use of nature was a deconstructed update of Art Nouveau's reworking of natural forms and that it presaged a fusing of forms both natural and everyday with the exotic and the luxurious. A prominent author of children's books said that she would soon release a tale about the *Princesse e le Escargot.* The following season, a play opened in Montmartre called *The Princess and the Snail.*

When they returned to Madame Lescaux's hat shop three days after their lesson, the hatmaker's eyes opened wide and brimmed with tears. She told them how much publicity the shop had gotten and how she had hundreds of requests for the hat. Kit granted Madame Lescaux the exclusive right to reproduce her design, with, of course, a share negotiated for Kit, by her manager, Lily. Years later, this would pay for a significant portion of her college tuition.

That summer in Paris became known as The Summer of the Snail. Knockoff fashion concerns put out cheap imitations of the snail hat, but if you were lucky, you had the real thing with the hand-embroidered label sewn on the inside that said,

"Madame Lescaux, design by Kit Maxwell."

On returning to Brooklyn, Kit wore her hat and T-shirt to school on her first day back. She got some curious looks on the walk to school, but in New York, people seemed too busy to really notice. At school, her friend Maddy Wingfield looked her up and down and declared, "You look absolutely hideous, Kit! Where did you get that goofy hat?"

Kit laughed and for once really didn't care what Maddy said about her clothes. "Ah, but of course it looks hideous to you, Maddy-moiselle. It was made in Paris especially for me!"

IV

Barcelona: Kit Up, Up and Away

On the brink of her teens, Kit was given the choice of where the family would travel while she was 12. She had seen some pictures of Gaudi's church of the Sagrada Familia, of the Casa Mila and the Casa Batllo, and she liked the colorful modern painting of Joan Miro, so she chose Barcelona. On earlier family trips, she had been the leader, the explorer, the scout who came back with new information. Now she was ready to explore herself, to keep a little part for herself. And she got something more than she expected.

Rome had shown her grandeur, Paris elegance, and Venice sheer originality. In Barcelona she found magic: she learned to fly and to change colors.

It started on the first day when the nine members of the family left the apartment they had taken in the Gracia neighborhood and took the funicular up the side of the mountain to the amusement park at Tibidabo. From there, they could see all across the city to the sea, with the mountains rising up at their backs and Montjuic, the mountain within the city, off to the right. Tibidabo has a new and an old amusement park. The new one presents the modern rides of a Six Flags or a Disney park, while the other is an old-school carnival with carousels, bumper cars, and Ferris wheels as likely to please Kit's grandparents, even if they didn't go on any rides, as the kids. But kids with a sense of history, wise souls like Kit, Lily, and Mia, tuned into the past with a palpable sense of excitement. They grasped the exoticism of the old, the nature of going back in time in a place like this, of channeling the worlds of their parents and their grandparents, even if they happened to be in a foreign country.

Furthermore, the new amusement park cost a lot for a day ticket, while you could go on the older rides one by one. So the cousins, Mia and Lily, and Kit and her father, Will, decided to each take a red airplane on the old airborne contraption. They made this determination despite the fact that not too many years ago, there had been a horrible accident on the ride, when people died. They reasoned that it had to be a lot safer now, that things on which accidents had happened were usually checked and watched closely after that to make sure nothing ever happened again. The ride sent Kit and Will dangling off the edge of the mountain, swinging from a cable out over the great city below. As they whirled around in widening arcs, Kit caught her cousins out of the corner of her eye, saw them laughing and screaming with delight.

From a young age, Kit had dreamed of going up into space, of breaking out of the pull of gravity, entering into orbit, into floating outer space. She had spacesuits and models of all the classic NASA ships. Now she felt like she was shot into space, could fly out over the menagerie of Barcelona, out over the four towers of the Sagrada Familia in the distance, down the broad boulevards of the Passeig de Gracia and the Ramblas down through the ancient Gothic Quarter to the wide blue expanse of the Mediterranean in the distance and out to sea and off the edge of the horizon and all the way over to Italy. She felt this without even closing her eyes. She was airborne, skyborne, navigating between the sun and the water, between the sun and the land. She waved to Rome, turned left and waved to Venice. She banked further to the north and over France, waving to the Eiffel Tower and Notre Dame in Paris. Then she headed back down over the Pyrenees into Spain again and finally came back to Earth. Her father and her coasted to a stop. She looked over at him with wide eyes, as if she didn't recognize him for a moment, as if she didn't know where she was. She smiled. She giggled. "Oh, Papa."

"Pretty great, huh? Did you enjoy that?" From the amusement park they made their way back down on the funicular. Kit was getting the sense in Barcelona that she would always be going up and coming back down, scaling to the top of a building or a mountain, riding or walking down, or maybe just flying around for a while. The whole crew strolled over through the handsome houses and little plazas of Gracia, over to Gaudi's Parc Guell, built originally to be a residential community, then turned into a park, and now, because of its important architectural identity, a museum of sorts.

The Parc is perched partly up the mountainside that cups the city into half of a bowl. They entered at their appointed reservation time and made their way around the grounds of mushroom-shaped columns and undulating staircases and finally reached the upper level with the serpentine park bench that snakes along for hundreds of feet. It's made of multicolored mosaic of tile, broken and pieced back together in rhythmic patterns, swooping lines, and vaguely connected suggestions of forms of things that might have derived from nature, maybe plants or rocks or something else. "It's the longest park bench in the world," Kit told Lily and Mia.

From there, they could still look out over the city, just about half way down the incline from where they had been in Tibidabo. "This is amazing," whispered Mia, struck by the melding of blue sky, the blue sea, the mountains to either side, and the shapes of the city below.

The air was chilly in the early spring. Kit bent over from her sitting position and laid her face directly on the mosaic tile. It was cool to the touch against her cheek. She closed her eyes. She felt that the insides of her body were made up of a mosaic of colors. There was oxblood red and Mediterranean blue, sunshine yellow and terracotta orange-brown, deep-space purple and falcon green, and the white of sand. She felt the colors pulse through her and lift her spirits off the bench into the air above her. She sat up and blinked. "Wow, this is cool," she said.

"You OK?" said Mia.

"I am more than OK," Kit smiled. "I am uplifted. I am a mosaic."

"You certainly are!" said her father.

The next day they took two taxis up Montjuic to the museum showcasing the work of the painter Joan Miro. The colors there reminded Kit of the bench. "See these shapes in his abstract paintings?" said her uncle, John. "Some people say that as a young man, Miro went to the Parc Guell and sat on the bench, and these lines, this rhythm in his paintings, come from those visits."

"Do you think the shapes stand for something?" asked Lily.

"I'm not sure. Like in some of them, I think it is a stand-in for something specific, like a red or orange shape like a circle represents the sun. But other times, I'm not sure it isn't more like just a shape that he liked."

"But still a profound shape," said Kit.

"Like maybe you can make what you want to out of it," said Mia.

"That's right," said her mom, Jenna. "With abstract art, there's a lot you have to bring to viewing it, it's open-ended, so it becomes a lot about you, too."

From the sculpture garden part of the museum they could look out over the city and back up to where they were the day before. Kit eyed an imaginary line shooting out from where she stood and leading all the way up to Tibidabo and her plane ride; then she turned her head and her laser view shot across the city to the bench in the Parc Guell. She felt connected to those places on the other side of the city.

They all left the Miro Foundation, enraptured by the painter's odd shapes and bold colors, and hiked up the winding road to where cable cars take off from the mountain and lead back down to the waterfront on the harbor far below. Suspended from a thin wire, looking out of the cable car into the sunshine, Kit felt on top of the world, the spring air running through her, not feeling superior to the Earth below, but connected to everything, nimble and sharp, ready to swoop down and enter the life below after the cleansing breeze of the view had brought everything into sharp focus.

"Look, Papa, we were flying over there, yesterday!"

"That's right, KitKat, pretty crazy!" They disembarked down by the docks and got some lunch at one of the seafood joints in the old fishermen's quarter of Barceloneta. Kit and Lily agreed they had never eaten shrimp so fresh before.

After lunch, they walked into the Gothic Quarter and explored the narrow medieval streets lined with shops and restaurants in the old stone buildings. There were emporiums selling rope-soled espadrilles, finely wrought wooden toys, messenger bags made from vinyl museum banners. But one storefront caught the attention of the three girls and wouldn't let go; it was called El Rey de la Magia, or the King of Magic, one of the conjuring shops in the old town. All nine members of the family crowded into the anteroom to watch the magician do her tricks. She would willingly demonstrate anything that you saw on display. Then, if you purchased it, she took you behind a curtain and showed you how it worked. She made things vanish into a set of wooden boxes with Asian carvings, linked together seemingly seamless rings of steel, turned a blank card deck into all aces and then a full deck of 52, and manipulated a gleaming silver set of cups so that knit-covered cork balls appeared to pass through the bottoms from one to another.

However, Kit was most interested in pure sleight of hand, hand magic that purported to be simpler, yet proved more baffling to the viewer than a magic contraption no one had ever seen before. She was drawn to the silk color-changing trick. The woman held up a purple silk, grasping the top two corners in a pinch with the index fingers and thumbs of each hand. Then she dropped the corner in her left and made an empty fist with her left hand. Bringing her right hand up with the handkerchief she pushed the first corner of purple into the top of her fist with her right pointer finger. Then she reached down to the bottom of her closed left hand and gently tugged out a peeking yellow corner from the bottom. Bit by bit, she transformed the purple to the yellow until she pulled the last bit out of her clenched fist.

They all eyed her hand suspiciously, thinking they had found her out, until she slyly and casually opened it to reveal nothing. All eyes went to her other hand which held nothing but the newly yellow scarf. She wore short sleeves. Kit was all in for this, and went behind the curtain, vowing, in the spirit of magicians everywhere, not to tell the others what she learned. The magician explained that it was all about timing and misdirection. It was not as much that the original purple silk ended up in her right hand, but that it was spirited away to who knows where well before the trick was over and long before the viewer even had a chance to shift concentration from that last bit of yellow being completely pulled out of the left hand.

Kit loved the simplicity of this, and found she could make the moves, and the ruse, even with her 12-year-old hands. Later, while they had hot chocolate at the Qatre Gats café, she performed it again, going backwards this time from yellow to purple; people at the nearby tables looked on and couldn't figure it out. The magician had given her an assortment of other silks to vary the colors: Mediterranean blue, oxblood red, terracotta, sandy white, falcon green.

They walked over to the base of the Ramblas and the girls were confounded by the statue of Columbus. "They sort of claim him here, though he was clearly an Italian," said John.

"Well, why do we have a statue of him at Columbus Circle?" asked Mia.

"That's a really good question," said her father. "He was an Italian who conquered Mexico, Cuba, Puerto Rico for the Spanish crown. And we are talking about the Spanish crown that settled in Madrid, not Barcelona."

"Ferdinand and Isabel," said Kit.

"Yes, so why do we have it in New York?" said Jenna. No one could answer that.

They turned off the Ramblas and walked through the lowest part of the Raval neighborhood to the church of San Pau de Camp. "This is the oldest church in Barcelona," said John. "It's the only one here built in the Romanesque style. There are lots of those in the mountains around here. They had a big influence on Gaudi and the other architects of his generation." The group entered the old church from an entrance room made of stone. They walked across a cloister lit by the bright Mediterranean sun and into the main part of the church, entering from the side.

"Look!" said Lily. The small, high windows cut into the stone in the Romanesque style sent two shafts of sunlight down across the nave and into the transept on the other side. The nine of them were the only ones in the old church. Lily took Kit's hand and led her across through the benches to the other side. "Stand here." She stood Kit so that her face was spotlighted in the beam of light. "Look up!" She looked into her camera and shot several pictures of the illuminated Kit. "Cool, you look like a goddess!"

Kit stood to the side and looked up along the sunbeam streaming down into the church. "Lily, do you think you could fly up this beam into outer space?"

"Well, it looks really solid, like a solid thing."

"Yeah, I think I'd like to ride it up." Kit pondered. "The only problem is, when you went through the hole in the wall of the church and came out above it, there really wouldn't be any beam of light anymore. I mean it would be there, but you wouldn't be able to see it in all the other beams of light in the sunshine, so I think maybe you would just fall down. I mean if you were riding the sunbeam that far, in the first place."

"That's an excellent point." said Mia.

They walked out of the church and through the narrow barrio of the Raval, filled with fruit vendors and discount appliance shops. An older man in a turban standing in front of a small storefront asked them if they would like to get their fortunes told.

"Can we, Mama?" said Lily. Lily's grandmother didn't love the idea. Why spend money, she said, and it could be creepy if you didn't know anything about the fortune teller. But her husband pointed out that they wouldn't say anything horrible if you were giving them your money and they were on vacation, so they decided to let the three girls have their fortunes told.

The space inside was only big enough for one person to enter; the other eight of them loitered outside on the street in the Raval, like they were waiting in line for a matinee. The woman inside wore a long gown with a headdress. She motioned to

Mia to sit down on the chair opposite her and studied her palm. "You have a wonderful spirit," she said. "You are a joy to those around you." Mia emerged from the little space and socked her mother on the arm.

"I am such a joy to you! She speaks the truth!" Lily sat down next. She felt like the woman looked deep into her eyes as she held her palm.

"You are very aware of your surroundings, like a cat. You notice what others miss."

John thought this assessment was spot on, but cautioned against any serious acceptance of the occult.

"Sometimes people doing this kind of thing are very perceptive, very clever about picking up on your personality, so I'm not so sure that was written on your palm," he said.

Kit went third. The woman studied her face and held her hand. Without really looking much at her palm, she said, "You are very intelligent. You are going through changes. Soon you will discover new things, secrets will be revealed to you." Kit walked out with a look of satisfaction on her face.

"I'll take it! She said I'm going to discover some sort of secrets! Bring it on!" They wandered back over near the Ramblas and into the vast grilled metal building housing the Boqueria market. There, they saw all kinds of food on display from spreads of every grade of *jamón ibérico* to stands selling unfamiliar varieties of cut-up fruits and their juices to arrays of all kinds of powdered spices in seemingly huge amounts in white plastic buckets.

"I mean, how much turmeric do they sell in a day?" said Kit's mom. There was a candy stand 15 feet across and 6 feet high with a rainbow palette as impressive for the bright intense colors of the gummies, sticks, divinities, flavored chocolates, and marbled halvah as any suggestion of their tastes beyond a tooth-hurting sweet. There were whole fish and swimming lobsters, lots of recently living things with their heads still on.

"You know," said Kit's dad. "I don't eat all this stuff, but this is really cool. This is something we really don't have in Brooklyn." They made their way out onto the Ramblas. Kit, Lily, and Mia gravitated over to one of the vendors selling live birds. They were red and blue and yellow.

"Look, Papa!" said Kit. She thought about letting the birds out so they could fly up and down the broad, divided esplanade of the Ramblas. She asked if they could take one home.

"No," said her father with a laugh. "I don't think that would fly with Dottie," the family puppy.

They reached the Placa de Catalunya and boarded a bus for the Sagrada Familia. "You know what?" said Kit. "I like it how we go up and up and then down and then down, and then after all that, they have a big street called the Diagonal so you can go sideways. That is really cool."

The Sagrada Familia made a grand impression on all of them. But the huge tourist crowds were distracting, the hordes of vendors selling souvenirs, the crowds from all over the world taking selfies, and the protocol of their scheduled visit. They all agreed it was amazing, but Mia said it kind of seemed like a haunted house. "That's right," said Jenna. "Since they've been building it for over a hundred years, it doesn't feel like a lot of religion has gone on here, like services, the way you feel that in the old church of San Pau, especially when it was so empty."

"Wow, a hundred years?" said Lily.

"Yeah, even a little longer than that. They might finish it sort of soon, in decades at least. The architect, Gaudi, died in 1926, and they've pretty much followed his plans for ninety years," explained Jenna. They left the church and walked up the broad promenade carved across the grid of the city streets that leads up to the Hospital San Pau. The city planners had effected this pairing, the huge strange church of the Sagrada Familia towering at one end, and then sitting at the other end of this diagonal slash across the streets, the 360 acres of the hospital, consisting of several dozen buildings built in the Barcelona *Modernisme* style with colored tile turrets rising above cornices lined with sculpture, red Catalan brick arched around windows, doors, arcades in a variegated pattern of styles: Arabic, Asian, Gothic, Romanesque, Classical.

They took a tour around the complex, and the guide explained how the different buildings housed different things—pediatrics over here, infectious diseases in a different place—all connected by tunnels underneath. How the architect, Domenech i Montaner, traveled around Europe a century ago to study hospital design before coming up with his plan.

"When great-grandpa died, was it in a place like this?" asked Kit.

"No," said Will. "That would have been sweet."

"Yeah, this would be a good place to be sick, if you had to be." she said. "It's kind of like a magic trick. Like they use all the color to trick you into thinking you feel better, and then you actually do."

"That's a nice thought, KitKat."

That evening, they attended a Spanish guitar concert at the Palau de la Musica Catalan, also designed by Domenech i Montaner, and Kit had the same feeling. With the complex colored glasswork and mosaic on the huge ceiling, the sculpture around the portico of the stage, "you would never know if the music was bad! Not that it was!" she said.

On the following day, Kit and her dad were walking along the middle esplanade of the broad Ramblas de Catalunya, dotted with sidewalk cafes and pedestrian benches in between the two avenues of car traffic. They were on their way to the grocery store when Kit spotted something on the ground. "Look, Papa, I think somebody dropped something!" She stooped and picked up an old-fashioned worn wallet. They looked around to see if it might have just been dropped. Her father pulled out an identification card and read an address on the very street they were on. Up the block they spotted a man with a shopping bag walking away from them. "Maybe it was his," said Kit, pointing.

They followed down the block, but he was into the next block before they had to stop at the crosswalk. They saw him enter a building on the left. When they approached, Will checked the address on the ID card and said, "I think we have our man." They looked into the foyer but didn't see anyone. Will rang the bell of the apartment at 5D. A man's voice came back, and Will said in the little Spanish he knew, *"Tenemos una bolsa,"* using the word for "purse" he had heard his wife use. *"Es de usted?"* There was a pause at the other end and then some unintelligible words. Then the buzzer sounded to let them in. They entered a lush marble lobby with an ornate metal elevator with fleur de lis and vinework enveloping the cage. "Do we get into that thing?" said Kit.

"I think so," said her father uncertainly. They stepped into the inside and Will pulled the sliding door shut. "Here we go." He pushed five and the elevator rose laboriously through five floors. They felt like they were going up into an historic shrine. When they reached the fifth floor, Kit was relieved. A door opened down the hall, and an older gentleman stuck out his head.

"Por favor, si us plau," he said, using both Spanish and Catalan.

"I'm sorry, we are Americans, English?" Will said, walking toward the man.

"Ah, yes, *un poco*, I know a little," he said. "Please, please come in." Will handed the wallet to him. "*Por dios*, thank you, thank you!" he said. "You have saved my life. It is everything important." Kit and Will walked down a long hallway and into a living room of sorts. Kit squinted and adjusted her eyes to the gloom. All around were stacks of papers, books, drawings, large folders, and models of things. She felt like they had happened upon the basement of a forgotten library. "Please, sit down," said the man. "I don't have much to offer you. Would you like some tea?"

"Oh no, we are fine, we just had breakfast," said Kit's dad.

"We were just going to the store and my daughter found your wallet out in the center of the Ramblas de Catalunya." The old man turned to her.

"Thank you so much. You are my little savior!" Kit smiled. It felt to her like no one had ever visited his apartment before.

"No problem. What is all this stuff?" she said. Will put his hand on her knee and frowned.

"Ah, it is OK," said the man. "I know it looks like a mess. It has come to be the time for me to give it all away."

"But what is it?" said Kit.

"It is the papers of my father. He was an architect here in Barcelona. One of the originals of the *Modernisme* style. I have his drawings, his plans for architecture, his notebooks, his models."

"Wow. Did he pass away?" she asked innocently, knowing his father would have to be, like 150 now.

"Yes, yes, he died in 1949. He was in poor health," said the man, as if his father had died the previous year.

"What did he build?" said Kit. Will winced but let her go on.

"Oh, he built some buildings down near Tarragona, where he was born, and some buildings in a suburb on the outskirts of Barcelona."

"Tarragona is a city to the south along the coast," Will told Kit.

"But he is most known for the work he did with Gaudi."

"Really? Did he work on the Sagrada Familia?"

"No, not really, but I do have a model of the church he or Gaudi made in the early days. Come, I'll show you." He led them into an adjacent room and there on a table stood a model of the church.

"There's one of those in the museum at the church," said Kit.

"Yes, that's right, but he did not work on it. He worked on the Casa Mila and the Casa Batllo around the corner from here. And up in the Parc Guell. Have you been up there? He made the bench."

Kit stared. "He made the bench up in the Parc Guell?"

"Well yes, he had workmen, of course, a crew, and instructions from Gaudi, but he made it, composed it like a work of art." He pulled out a scrapbook and showed Kit some pictures. Some showed his father working on the park bench in old photographs. "This is from the first decade of the last century. And here are some pictures of some of his own buildings." He showed her a photo of a house with bulbous turrets in blue and white tile, with metal balconies interspersed. "They called this the Egg House, for its shape." Kit's eyes opened wide.

"How come you have all of his stuff here in your apartment? I mean, wouldn't they want it at the college or the museum at the Parc Guell?" The man let out a deep sigh.

"Yes, you are right. It is time I need to give it away. There are scholars and architects who want to see it all. People who study Gaudi. People who study my father."

"Why have you held onto it?" Kit asked innocently.

The architect's son smiled painfully. "Well, I grew up here in this apartment with my father and mother. They both died long, long ago. During the civil war, my father hid priests here. He was a very religious man. But he didn't like Franco." He paused and considered. "I feel like if I part with all of his stuff, I will just be an old man in an empty apartment. The vultures are circling and when they take everything, all that will be left is this old, how do you say, carcass."

Kit looked up at him in sympathy. "But they will want to talk to you about your father... forever," she stammered.

"Yes, that is true. You have a wise daughter there, sir," he said gravely.

"Well, she certainly has some sharp eyesight," said her dad. "I'm glad she found your wallet and that we could be of some service to you."

"Oh, you have saved me! My identity card! It is the key to my pension and my life." He turned to Kit. "I would like to give you something. I don't have much."

"Oh, that's all right," said Will.

"Wait a moment," he said and left the room. He came back

in a minute with a small sealed brown envelope. "When my father made the bench, he used a, how do you say it, technique, called *trencadís*. He broke up cups and saucers and plates and such and glued them back together to make the mosaic on the bench. Here are a few of the pieces he didn't use."

Kit took the envelope with her eyes open wide. "These are pieces from the bench? Are you sure I can have them?"

"Well these are ones he didn't use. And yes, you can have them. I have many many more. You reminded me it is time to clean it out, to give it away. This is the start. Thank you for finding my wallet and bringing it to me. You are the first people to come here in a while. This is all I can do to repay you."

"There's the secret you found, KitKat."

"Thank you so much!" said Kit. They left the old gentleman to his solitude, opting this time not to take the elevator. Kit bound down the five flights of marble stairs winding around the cage of the lift. She couldn't wait to open the envelope. Out on the street, with their errand still to accomplish, she implored her dad, "Papa, can I sit down here and open this? I really, really want to see what's inside."

"Sure, let's do it. I'm curious, too. That is really something he gave you." Kit sat on one of the benches in that broad middle section of the Ramblas de Catalunya. Her hands were trembling as she carefully unsealed the envelope, not wanting to tear it and lose anything. She dumped the contents into her palm. There she found bits of broken ceramic in colors she knew: oxblood red, Mediterranean blue, sunshine yellow, terracotta, deep-space purple, falcon green, sandy white.

"Look, Papa, these are over a hundred years old."

"That's unbelievable, Kit. Everyone in Barcelona probably wants to know what's inside that apartment and now you have part of it." Kit felt again like she could fly down the boulevard across the Gran Via onto the lower Ramblas, down to the shore, and out over the sea. The little bits of broken crockery made her feel special in a way she could not explain.

Later that day, she and her parents went for a walk. They landed at the top of the Ramblas looking down the street. They saw the memorials to the victims of the 2017 terrorist attacks when people had been run down by a van, now remembered in chalk-inscribed messages and with clusters of candles. The vendors of colored birds were interspersed with the sacred remembrances. Kit grabbed the hands of both her parents on either side of her. "I love you," she said.

"Kit, that's so sweet, we love you, too!" said her mom.

"Thank you for bringing me here and for being my parents," she said, quite seriously.

"Of course, there's nothing else we would be doing instead, my love," said her mom. Her father looked at her evenly and said:

"We are still NOT buying you a bird."